A Touch of the Son
Copyright©2012 Barry Lowe
ISBN 978-1-911478-19-5
Cover art and design by Dawné Dominique

A Touch of the Son was originally published by loveyoudivine Alterotica and includes – Man Of The Hour, Like Father Like Son, Sonny & Shared, Sonny Side Up, Eclipse Of The Son, Son & Games, Where the Son Don't Shine, The Son Shines Out of His Ass, and Have Son, Will Travel – all previously published as individual eBooks by loveyoudivine Alterotica.

Published by
Lydian Press 2017
Find us on the World Wide Web at
http://www.lydianpress.com

A TOUCH OF THE SON

Barry Lowe

Lydian Press

Contents

Page:

   1   Man Of The Hour

  23   Like Father Like Son

  55   Sonny & Shared

  95   Sonny Side Up

117   Eclipse Of The Son

151   Son & Games

173   Where the Son Don't Shine

197   The Son Shines Out of His Ass

225   Have Son Will Travel

Their secret passion will lead them to hell.
Will they be able to find their way back?

MAN OF THE HOUR

$\mathcal{I}$ swore out loud, and got my reward in a number of withering glares from passing adults with children. Abashed, I mumbled an apology but I was seriously pissed off having taken precious time from my busy schedule to come to the airport to pick up my son only to discover his flight had been delayed and was not due for two hours. Not enough time to get to the city and back.

I briefly toyed with the idea of chucking the whole pick-up business aside to let my secretary do the honors, leaving me time to investigate several important management problems that were bugging me. She loved kids and I had no doubt my son would much prefer a hot twenty-three-year-old babe for a meet-and-greet than his almost forty-year-old gay dad. Not that I don't like kids. Just not my own.

Our last meeting had been anything but auspicious. He'd been fourteen and a stuck-up twat who'd just learned about my sexual predilection from his mother who'd revealed all in an effort to drive yet another wedge into our non-existent relationship. I suppose she had every right to be angry with me since the afternoon she'd come home early from her job as a nurse at the local hospital to catch me with my prick buried up the ass of the very cute college student who supplemented his income by moonlighting as a pizza delivery boy. And, God, did he deliver!

One pizza with everything equals messy divorce, plus losing custody of our two-year-old son, Jason, who'd been spending the night at his grandma's which is why I'd decided to lash out and experiment with my gay side. I'd suspected for a long time that I might swing both ways but after one night with Mr. Pizza, I defected to the opposing team. Full time.

My wife moved away to a small town on the other side of the country, spurred on by my infidelity and dissatisfaction with city life in general. It brought out the redneck in her and she, in turn, passed it on to my son who contacted me rarely and then only via email. They became few and far between. The few attempts at visitation rights had been rebuffed with the suggestion a visit would not be looked upon with favor by either my wife's new husband or any of their redneck friends who regularly referred to me as 'The Faggot' in front of my son.

It didn't hurt as much as it could have because I threw myself into my new-found sexuality with the sort of missionary zeal that comes with conversion. My embrace of my new religion saw me worshipping at the altar of cock and male ass at every opportunity, whether it be in bars, back rooms or the open air splendor of public parks. I never let a chance slip by, indifferent as I was to color, creed, age, body shape, or political affiliation. I was a sucker for any man's cock, and any man's ass was fair game as far as I was concerned. Over time, and much experimentation however, I learned that there was one physical type that got my gonads churning like no other: college-age boys in their early twenties.

They were so special I had even allowed a few of them to tap my ass.

Now I was waiting for my own college-age brat, the antithesis of all I held horny. A non-athletic book botherer, a worrier not a warrior. A self-opinionated, homophobic pimple-faced blight on humanity. And they expected me to ease his way into the local college. After he had humiliated me, and my friends, by referring to us as 'fags' at the age of fourteen when I'd last seen him. His three-week stay then had been an unmitigated disaster and led to total estrangement. I loathed the little bastard and his efforts to denigrate me and my 'chosen lifestyle.' Initially, I welcomed the opportunity of rapprochement, hoping for a little dad/son bonding. If anything, it drove us farther apart. Especially when he boldly informed me that he would lock his bedroom door at night and if he so much as heard me breathe outside his door, he would call the police.

The final straw was the night he called me a 'fat faggot slug' in front of a man I had been trying to impress for almost a year. I had finally succeeded in getting him to my home only to be humiliated by my son, a veritable little Billy Bunter himself. His name calling had one good result, I took up exercise and the gym. The little bastard would hardly recognize me now. We'd see who had the last chuckle over body weight.

Once he returned to his mother, confirming her conviction that I was the anti-Christ, I never kept in touch. Not on birthdays, not on Christmas, not on any occasion of importance in his life. If he had any. For all emotional purposes, he was dead to me.

That's why it was surprising when I got the phone call from my former wife. Our dealings were usually lawyer to lawyer. I was about to hang up on her when I realized her first words were not the usual, "Hello, faggot" of our infrequent phone conversations. I put the phone back to my ear.

"What do you want, Irene?"

"It's our son," she said hesitantly.

I wasn't even father enough to get that tight clutch around my heart that something may have happened to him.

"Oh, he's our son now after he's been your son for how long now? Eighteen years?"

She turned my sarcasm back on me. "He's twenty. Almost twenty-one."

"How much is this going to cost me, Irene?"

I had paid alimony without missing a week until he turned eighteen. Thereafter, I had paid, no questions asked, for 'incidentals' that she passed on via legal representation. This must be a whopper if she felt the need to ring me personally.

I heard her sigh down the phone. Now we were getting to the point. "Look, Buzz."

It must be serious; she was using her pet name for me that she never uttered outside the bedroom. I got it because I always wore my hair in a buzz cut. Back then at any rate.

"The sooner you spit it out Irene, the sooner we can put an end to this painful conversation and get back to our respective lives." I guess I was more brutal than was necessary. "This is the first time you've spoken to me in what is it, seven or eight years, since you foisted that nasty little fourteen-year-old sprog on to me. And you know how well that went."

She sounded as if she were about to disagree but must have thought better of it.

"He wants to visit again, Buzz."

I groaned. "Christ, Irene. What for?"

"He's got a scholarship to the college where you are. The only one he could get."

I found that difficult to imagine as he never had his nose out of a book. He wasn't exactly the athletic type. By now, he must be goggle-eyed from study. It's all he did during his three-week stay with me. That, and turn insults into an Olympic sport.

"And?"

"He wants to stay with you until he can find accommodation and settle in. We're not wealthy people, Buzz."

She was playing every blackmail card at her disposal.

"He won't be any trouble," she said after a long pause.

"I'm not changing my lifestyle for the little shit," I said, mentally calculating what I would have to do to make my home non-threatening to a twenty-year-old heterosexual boy. There, I'd already reneged on the promise I made myself the day I pushed his fourteen-year-old butt through the departure lounge gate wiping my hands of him and vowing I would never compromise myself for anyone in the future. Now I was doing that very thing.

"You don't have to. He won't be there long."

"Why couldn't he have found a college closer to you?"

"Look, there's no use moaning over what's done. He's your son, although I admit, you've never done anything to show it. You owe him this much."

"I don't owe him squat," I said, close to yelling, then calmed down. "Okay, if it's only until he gets himself acclimatized to the big scary city and finds somewhere to stay, I'll put up with him, but…" I paused to gather my thoughts. "But, he has to obey a few rules this time."

"I'm sure that will be no problem. As long as you and your mates keep your hands to yourselves."

That was low even for Irene. I hung up the phone on her but she rang straight back. I was tempted not to answer although that would have been childish. As punishment, I did let it ring for the longest time. That gave me time to get my rage under control and actually chuckle at the thought of any of my friends even contemplating a tryst with my lard-assed flabby son.

"I'm sorry, Buzz," she said, "That was uncalled for."

I put my foot down. "I'll agree to this on one condition."

"That is?"

"He show some respect. Okay, he doesn't have to like the fact his old man is gay, but I will not tolerate him calling me and my friends 'fags' in my own home."

"He did that?" Irene sounded genuinely surprised.

"As if you didn't know."

She went to interrupt but I kept right on. "I will do everything in my power to help the ungrateful bastard. I expect...I *want* nothing in return. But he will not disrespect me."

"He called you names?"

"Oh, like you didn't know, Irene. I wonder where he got it from. Could it be from you and that redneck husband of yours? Like you said, it's in the past, let's leave it there."

She must have decided withdrawal was the best solution and after giving me his flight details and his mobile phone number, she hung up.

That's why I was at the airport; grinding my teeth after discovering his flight had been delayed. I rang his mobile but it was switched off so I left a message asking him to call me to let me know if he was on the next flight. I decided to have a coffee and ring the office to see if there was anything urgent that required my attention.

There was a small café nearby that sold my favorite brand of heart starter and the tables gave me a perfect view of the Arrivals board. My secretary informed me, with the sort of superiority to her voice that suggested a raise in pay would be welcome, that she was perfectly capable of holding down the fort in my absence, and that there was nothing urgent that needed my attention. To while away the time, I got myself a coffee and some sort of non-descript pastry that hadn't seen the inside of an oven for days and which, at airport prices, cost the equivalent of a meal downtown. I took one bite of the flavorless sawdust before pushing it across the table, to concentrate on the coffee, which was as good as the pastry was stale. No point in wishing I'd thought to bring my laptop with me. Instead, I settled for a newspaper, yesterday's as it turned out, flipping to the business opportunities at the back. I still had ninety minutes or more to fill in.

I was engrossed in the comics when a shadow fell across the table.

"Personally, I don't think comics have survived the retirement of Bill Watterson. I miss *Calvin and Hobbes*."

My interest was piqued. Watterson's strip had been a guilty pleasure and I had a bookshelf lined with his comic omnibuses at home. I'd always wished Jason had been more like Calvin.

"Is this seat taken?" he asked.

He took my lack of a response as a rejection. But he was wrong. I'd been gobsmacked by his beauty.

"Sorry, man, I didn't mean to disturb you." He began to move away.

He hadn't disturbed me. Well, perhaps, my libido had been disturbed.

"Sorry, where are my manners. Please, sit down."

He smiled, pulled out the chair, and sat gracefully, giving me an eyeful of a packed crotch that promised nirvana, and a body scarcely contained by a tight T-shirt that strained around his biceps and across his chest. My cock hardened instantly.

I folded my paper and leaned across the table, offering my hand. "My friends call me Buzz," I said.

His handshake was firm, without that aggression that some men feel they need to exude authority.

"I hope you'll count me as one of your friends, Buzz," he purred. If I wasn't an old cynic, I would have thought he was flirting with me. "I'm Cal. I guess my parents liked the strip as well."

"You want a coffee, Cal? I was about to get a refill."

He appeared embarrassed. "Look, I gotta be honest," he said. "One of the reasons I sat here was that neglected pastry. I thought I might be able to snatch it while you weren't looking."

I laughed. "You're either very poor or very hungry."

"Both," he interrupted.

"Be my guest," I said, pushing the plate toward him. "But let me warn you, it has seen better days. If it was a horse, they would have shot it."

He laughed then began to wolf it down. I guess I was a little disappointed that his interest was in my leftovers rather than in me, but I would never have followed up anyway.

"You want a coffee to go with that snack?" I said as I stood preparing to move to the counter. "My treat."

He mumbled something between crumbs which I took to be the affirmative.

When I got back to the table, he was picking up the last of the pastry flakes on the end of his spit slicked finger. I wondered how it would feel if it were my cock being pushed between his soft lips. I sat down as my cock tented in my jeans.

I pushed the coffee toward him. With a plate of sandwiches.

He looked at me.

"As I said, my treat."

He opened the cardboard packet and began to devour them greedily. "Thanks, man. Um… Buzz."

I wanted to soften the burden of accepting food from a stranger. "If you want to pay me back…"

I saw him stop chewing.

"Then maybe some time in the future when you find yourself in a similar situation, then remember this and be charitable to that someone who's down on his luck."

He relaxed, polishing off the sandwiches in record time, burping his appreciation.

"Sorry. Habit, I suppose. But they sure tasted fine."

He watched me closely as he sipped his coffee, leaning back contentedly. I was uncomfortable under his inquisitive gaze and glanced at the Arrivals board. "You waiting for someone?" he asked.

"Yeah. The plane has been delayed."

"How long?"

"I've got over an hour to fill in."

"That's good," he smiled, leaning closer. "There was another reason I wanted to sit here."

"What was that?" I asked.

"You're hot."

I spluttered my coffee. I'd never had a young man proposition me so openly. He pressed his knee against mine so I could feel his heat.

"And you're fuckin' gorgeous," I replied.

"So the only dilemma is where do we go to fill in a very pleasurable hour? They're not likely to let us into the First Class Lounge. Your car is probably too public. Right here on the table would get us arrested although I have been known to do it for an audience."

I groaned at the fantasy.

"You like that, eh?"

I nodded my head enthusiastically.

"In that case, follow me."

He was up from the table, shucking on his backpack, and striding away before I caught up with him.

"It was only a sandwich and a coffee. You don't have to do this," I said, taking his arm to slow him down.

He turned on me, his eyes flashing anger. "You think I'd fuck you for a crappy sandwich and stale Danish?"

I mumbled an apology. He calmed down.

"I get off on older dudes," he said. "Not ancients. But Daddy types. You know?"

I nodded.

"I thought you might get off on guys my age. I was hoping you were up for a bit of adventure. I guess I was wrong."

Fuck! I was going to lose him. My cock was screaming what a foolish old man I was.

"Nah," I said warmly. "I love fucking the ass off guys your age till they can't stand up. Just not used to them coming on so strong."

He smiled. "Life's too short to beat around the bush. You up for that adventure then?"

"Fuck, yeah," I said as he took off again.

I kept pace with him as I knew where he was headed. When we got there, he didn't even bother to look around but just opened the door as if he had every right to use it.

"Live dangerously, daddy," he said as he pulled open the door to the disabled toilet and ducked inside.

Following him without thinking, I locked the door behind us. The stall was much more spacious than an ordinary men's room cubicle and we had total privacy – unless someone came knocking on the door. I'd worry about that when it happened. Right now, I had more on my mind, like the handsome young man who wrapped me in his arms, thrusting his warm tongue into my mouth, sucking gently as he ground his crotch against mine. It was difficult to determine who was harder.

I glanced at my watch, remembering Jason was arriving shortly.

"Plenty of time, old man," Cal said as he sat on the toilet seat spreading his legs to reveal a very substantial bulge. "Come on, daddy. Strip for me. Show me what you've got."

I fumbled nervously with my shirt until he put his hand up for me to stop. "Come on, man. Tease me. Don't play this like some back-alley whore who wants it over and done with." He spoke like we had all the time in the world. I looked at my watch again. "Whoever it is you're meeting. Let them wait."

He was right. I owed nothing to the little turd who claimed fealty as my son. And short of a cannon or a battering ram we were perfectly safe in this room. Relaxing my shoulders, I imitated my idea of a stripper, undoing my shirt and dipping the collar over my shoulder to reveal a bit more flesh.

Cal whistled his appreciation. "Woo hoo, daddy, way to go."

Whipping the shirt off in a single movement that impressed even me I played with my nipples, pretending my tongue was long enough to lick them. I wish. I settled for squeezing them until they were hard as pebbles, swiveling my pelvis like a cut-price Elvis, as I squeezed my pecs together to make a channel deep enough for a cock hoping Cal might oblige later and leave me with a pearl necklace.

His face curled into an evil smile as he reached for his fly. I slithered over to him, beating his hand away, and then sat on his groin like some cheap pole dancer grinding into him until he was gasping. I kissed him with a force that he returned. We were two horny men looking to get our rocks off. When we came up for air, he clamped his mouth over my nipple biting down hard. Pain shot through me, ending up in my cock which twitched its appreciation.

Turning his attention to the other nipple, he repeated the exercise while fumbling with my belt, carefully unzipping me so that my cock sprang free.

"Commando style. I like that in a daddy," he smirked. "But I like this even more," He grabbed my cock and gave it a few perfunctory tugs before running his thumb across the piss slit, slimy with pre-cum. I pulled away, much too sensitive and much too close to losing my load.

I stood up to get away from his hands and my jeans fell down. I shucked off my heavy leather work boots, de rigueur for the construction sites I tramped over daily, and stripped. I was totally naked except for my socks.

"Put your boots back on," he whispered hoarsely.

I must have hesitated too long.

"Please," he begged.

I did as he asked, surprised how sexy I felt totally naked except for my boots.

"You look fuckin' amazing." To prove it he snuggled up against my body, running his hands across my skin, squeezing here, pinching there, and lingering over my pecs and my biceps as if they were national treasures. "You are one hot daddy."

He lifted my arm above my head, holding it there in order to caress my hairy armpit with his nose. His tongue snaked out, licking my sweaty pit, before he chewed on the matted hairs, sucking the funky skin. It tickled slightly but it was the most erotic thing anyone had done to me in ages. After he lathered one, he began on the other until I was so wild for him I couldn't stand it anymore. I grabbed his hair, pulling him away. I looked into his eyes and then crushed my mouth against his, tasting my pit funk and his spit.

I wanted him so bad.

"Sit where I was for a minute. I want to worship you."

He pushed me gently back to the toilet. I sat back, leaning against the cold steel plumbing, spreading my legs wide, my boots obscene reminders of my nakedness. His eyes ran over my body with the concentration of some scientist examining a bug under a microscope. I knew I had a decent body, I work out four or five times a week, and from the grin of satisfaction on his face he liked what he saw.

Still fully clothed, he kneeled on the cold tiled floor like a servile dog and began to lick my boots. I attempted to pull away but he held tight to my leg as he ran his tongue over the leather toe, spit slicking it until it started to shine. I twitched in anticipation of that mouth wrapping around my cock. Before he began work on my second boot, he sat up on his haunches and stripped his T-shirt over his head.

His body was magnificent. It made me look scrawny. He wasn't over-developed like some young guys who go overboard on steroids; still he was buff without an ounce of body fat that I could see. My cock oozed its appreciation.

"Holy fuck, Cal. You are one magnificent specimen, son. With that body and your looks you could have anyone you want."

I did wonder why he was here with me.

"Except the men I want," he said. "Guys like you are too afraid to approach me. Think I'll be too full of myself."

"Come here," I said.

He sat in my lap and I cradled him for a moment smoothing my hands over his back, suggesting there was more to this encounter than just a bit of wham/bam. When I thought he'd had enough mollycoddling I pushed him back down on his knees and planted my neglected boot in his crotch.

"Get to work, son. We haven't got all fuckin' day." I wished we had.

"Yes, sir," he said obediently, slavering over my leather boot.

How I wished I could keep him down there for hours, servicing my needs. I didn't dare look at my watch. I could only live for the moment.

"Okay, fucker. Time to polish daddy's balls," I tugged none-too-gently at his hair to get his attention where I wanted it and he didn't hesitate to lick my hairy ball sack before sucking each nut into his hot mouth to wash them with his spit. He didn't touch my shaft although his face brushed it from time to time in his enthusiastic worship of my body. He looked up at me like some cock slave, his eyes pleading. "Please," he whispered.

"You can kiss it."

That's all I allowed him, for my own protection rather than a lack of enthusiasm. It wouldn't take much to make me blow. He put his lips to the head of my cock, licking up the slime that had leaked out, but made no attempt to go further, even though I knew we both wanted him to.

"Right, son. Your turn. Show daddy what you got."

He stood and slowly peeled off his belt then unzipped his trousers to give me a glimpse of the prize underneath. He turned his back to shimmy out of his chinos and his briefs. There was method in his teasing because the most perfect ass I had ever seen confronted me. Sculpted perfection. Michelangelo could not have created anything as perfect. Cal knew it too. He swiveled his ass provocatively as a come on but I controlled myself.

"Turn around, son."

Cal swirled around to reveal his cock was no less perfect. Obviously excited by our encounter, he was leaking cum like oil from the engine on a clapped-out truck.

"You are fuckin' perfection. If I was fifteen years younger I'd carry you off…"

Realizing I was saying too much and in danger of ruining the scene I clammed up, covering my faux pas with a snapped command. "Over here fucker, back to me, grab your ankles."

His reaction was immediate and I had his butt in front of my face. Running my hands across it, I slapped his cheeks hard, making them red. Cal groaned his approval. I slipped my finger into his crack and found the damp entrance, playing with it awhile before prodding for admission. My finger sank in easily although he tightened up once my knuckle breached the entrance. He needed a little natural lubrication.

Pushing my face into the crack, I lapped at his hole just as he had at my pits and boots. I sucked and chewed, relaxing the tight muscle, probing with my tongue, to prepare it for my assault. He gasped each time I nibbled the entrance with my teeth.

"Fuck me, daddy. Please fuck me now," he whimpered. "I don't think I can last much longer."

I pushed him slightly forward to give me space to stand up before aiming my cock at his hole, pushing slowly, slipping in easier than I would have thought. I hesitated when I heard his sharp intake of breath. He reached around to pull me farther inside him.

"I like it when it hurts a bit, daddy," he explained. "Fuck me hard. So I never forget you."

I pulled my cock out fully before lining it up with his tight pink hole and then rammed my blunt instrument into the passageway. He shuddered from the assault. "Fuck!"

Panting, he pushed back against me, grinding his ass against my pubes and my balls, almost as if trying to suck my whole body inside him. I slid back and forth a few times, trying to embed my cock but with us standing precariously I couldn't fully get a grip so I spun him around to face the plumbing. He immediately saw my reasoning, and bent over to grip the toilet bowl then thrust his ass backward taking me to the hilt. Gripping his strong muscular waist, I began pounding into his hole, feeling his sphincter grip me every time I plunged forward.

"You are one fuckin' slut, son. I could ride your sweet asshole all day."

"Go for it, daddy. Tame my slut ass."

"I bet even your real dad would fuck you if he knew what you can do with your boy cunt. Shit! I've never had one better."

I'd planted the idea and it must have done his head in as he thrust back against me with more force than ever, enough that my balls would be black and blue in the morning. I reached under to tug on his nipples, distending them until I thought they'd snap like rubber bands. Still he ground against me, his insatiable ass demanding more.

I couldn't hold out much longer, sweat was pouring off my body, my chest damp with effort. Licking his back, biting it hard enough I left marks, I grabbed his balls pulling the sack tight and squeezing. He moaned, attempting to turn his head so I could kiss him. I tongued his chin and his lips as I wrapped my fist around his cock, milking it slowly using his own slime as lubrication.

"Fuck, daddy. I can't hold on much longer."

"That's okay, son," I panted. "Daddy has a load with your name on it. You ready, boy?"

"Breed my asshole, Fill me with daddy batter, man."

I straightened up in order to gain leverage to cram my prick inside him as far as it would go. A few more strokes like that would send me over the edge. Cal fisted his own weapon until I heard him grunt excitedly and felt the clench of his ass around my cock. I clutched his body, pulling him on to me while I shot my load deep inside him.

"Take it all you fuck slut. Feel daddy dump his spunk inside you, so deep you'll never get it out."

My squirts seemed to take forever as did the palpitations in his butt until I sagged onto his back, exhausted.

"Oh, man," he said. "That was wicked. So intense. I gotta meet up with you again. Do it properly next time."

I wasn't sure what 'properly' meant but I was eager to learn.

Pulling out slowly, my cock still sensitive, a dribble of sperm came with it. Looking down, I noticed his come had flecked my boots.

I slammed my foot on the bowl near his head which was still bowed from the effort of our fuck.

"I think you have some cleaning up to do, son."

"I'm fucked, daddy. Give me a break. I gotta go." He turned and smiled at me.

I read that smirk as a challenge, so I took it. I grabbed his hair roughly, mashing his face against the leather slimed with his spunk.

"You'll go when you clean up your mess, son. Now get that boot shining."

I smeared his face over my boot, his tongue darting out to savor his own spunk.

"Taste good, son?"

"Uh huh," he managed to say. "But I bet Daddy's tastes better."

I pulled his head up, forcing my semi-hard cock, slimy with my man slime and his ass juices, between his lips. He sucked, swallowing the nasty residue until I brought his face up to mine to kiss him, savoring our mingled spunk mixed with a slight flavor of boot polish.

"Good boy," I complimented him, slapping him on the ass as he bent to retrieve his trousers.

Once dressed we both looked respectable enough although anyone with a dirty mind would notice we wore the happy expression of the well fucked.

He stared at me uncomfortably for a moment before he blurted it out. "Look, I know this was a quick hook-up but you are so fuckin' tremendous, man. You know how to play the game and play it good. I don't do this often but, well, while I'm in town…"

He didn't finish the sentence so I had to. "That ass and that body are the best I've ever sampled. No bullshit. I ain't gonna let that go if I can help it. I want another opportunity to fully explore that body of yours. Maybe, even…" I grabbed his cock for emphasis and, as if in agreement, it began to harden. "But right now I gotta make a call, otherwise someone is gonna be right royally pissed off and will make my life a living hell. You go on ahead so no one sees us leaving the toilet together, I'll make my call, and I'll meet you back at the coffee lounge. Give you my details and get yours. Okay?"

He nodded agreement before disappearing out the door. I retrieved my mobile from my jeans pocket, slipping out myself and, even though no one was looking, I limped a little for the CCTV cameras that must be trained on the passageway. I saw Cal half-way across the terminal going toward our rendezvous point. I looked at the Arrivals board. Shit! Jason's plane had landed about half an hour before, much earlier than expected. I speed dialed the number his mother had given me praying he was still at the baggage carousel.

I heard a mobile ringing in the distance. I couldn't see him. It rang again. I saw Cal stop and retrieve his phone. I saw him press the answer button with a sense of dread.

"Jason?" I said.

Cal swung around and looked straight at me, his face a mask of horror.

"Dad?"

LIKE FATHER LIKE SON

"*Y*ou did what?"

"You heard what I said."

"You slept with a man you once described as, let me see if I can remember your exact words, 'a little fat slug that was an insult to the human genome pool?' I think I got that right."

I sighed, wondering why I had ever thought it was a good idea telling my best friend, Clive, what I'd done. Then I realized his was the most understanding ear I could bend. My straight friends of either gender would be horrified by my revelation and most of my gay male friends and acquaintances who weren't similarly grossed out, would be lining up to tap Jason's ass for themselves. So, Clive it was. I had to tell somebody, the secret was eating away at me.

He didn't pause for breath. "This is the same son who called us all fags and threatened the police on us if we so much as farted in his direction. The son who has all the personality of a puss-filled pimple, and looks exactly like the human embodiment of one as well."

I groaned. Yes, that's how I'd described him. Once. "That was when he was fourteen. He doesn't look like Billy Bunter anymore."

"Obviously."

"And I didn't sleep with him as you put it, I fucked him. There was no sleeping involved."

He saw my distress, and immediately adopted amateur psychologist mode. "How are you feeling?"

"Guilty as hell."

That's why I was at the gym, attempting to work off my stress and my guilt and, I had to admit it as much as I didn't want to, my excitement.

"Guilty? Why, if it was an accident?"

"Do I really have to spell it out? Because he's my own son. My own flesh and blood."

Clive showed his exasperation with a shrug and an escape of breath through tight lips. "You didn't know that at the time."

"But I know it now. Hence the guilt." I had to calm down, I was beginning to raise my voice, and other guys were staring at us.

"How's he?"

"That's the remarkable part. Doesn't seem to have fazed him a bit. In fact, he seems quite pleased with the whole exercise."

"Wow. So, leaving the guilt aside for the moment, how was it?"

I smiled. "You're an evil man, Clive."

"You know flattery doesn't work with me. Now, fess up."

"Before I knew who he was, allowing for the fact it was rushed and we did it in a toilet at the airport…" I hesitated, not to consider my reaction as I had run it through my head repeatedly since the incident, shuddering inwardly that I came up with the same answer every time, but because it was an answer I just couldn't deal with. "I'd give it twelve out of ten."

"He give the same score?"

I shrugged. "He's hinted he'd like a repeat."

"Shit. You do have a problem."

That was the understatement of the year.

At the airport, when I'd called my son's mobile only to have the stranger's phone ring we'd both been open-mouthed with shock then Cal laughed fit to burst and I joined in. We were still laughing when we reached the car and I stowed his backpack.

As I drove out of the car park toward the expressway back to the city, I had to ask, "So, Cal. Your plane got in early?"

"No, Buzz. I got to the airport early. When I discovered my flight was delayed, I begged them to get me on the earlier one. It was just boarding and because I had no luggage, well, you know the rest."

"Cal? Why Cal? If you'd used your real name I would have twigged."

"It is my real name. Remember. Middle initial C."

I had forgotten. Just like I'd forgotten everything about my son after his disastrous visit when he was fourteen.

"Buzz?"

"Your mum's nickname for me when we…"

"Ewww." He screwed up his nose in disgust.

"You didn't recognize me?" I asked.

"Did you recognize me?"

Touché. We'd both changed in the intervening years. I'd dropped thirty pounds. He'd grown up. I'd built up my body, he'd built up more.

Sighing, I admitted, "All I saw was a hot young man then my dick took over."

"I wasn't expecting my old man to scrub up like a walking horn dog."

There were so many questions, but I decided to save them for later. Right now, I'd drop him at the university to enroll and pick up the paperwork while I headed to the gym to pound the self-reproach out of my system. We could go over the day's momentous events this evening. Unless…

"Look, if you don't want to stay, if you're uncomfortable…"

"Dad, relax. I'm fine. It's no big deal."

We sat in silence while I ran through my head how I'd behaved, what I'd said, what the police would think when they came to arrest me, and – the damn images kept popping up in my head – how much I'd enjoyed it. My stiff cock kept emphasizing the point.

I glanced over at Jason relaxing in the passenger seat beside me. The amused smirk curling his lips made me wonder if he was thinking the same things I was. Something twitched in his trousers. I guess he was. Stunned, I looked away and concentrated on my driving.

The ensuing silence went on for so long it threatened to engulf us.

"Look, dad." Jason burst through my thoughts. "It's no big deal. We're both consenting adults. It's not like either of us knew, though I can only imagine how intense it would have been if we had." He moaned at the thought. "What I'm saying is, quit the stressing. You're giving me a headache so it must be hell up there for you." He tapped the side of my head for emphasis.

"Just proves your mother was right about me all along."

"Is that what this is all about?"

Was it? Fatherly instinct must be innate. I was worrying about things I'd never contemplated being a problem before. Then again, I'd never fucked my own son before either.

Jason took my lack of response as a 'yes.' "What? You think I'm gonna get on the phone and tell her, 'Hey, guess what, mum? Dad fucked me up the ass in a toilet at the airport just like you always warned me.' Yeah, right."

That was all the confirmation I needed that she'd been poisoning his mind against me all his life.

Jason powered down his window, sticking his head out to yell, "Hey, mum. Why didn't you tell me how fuckin' hot it would be to fuck my own dad?"

Other cars speeding along the expressway blared their horns at his behavior. I grabbed at him to drag him back inside, ending up with a handful of crotch.

He looked at me with those incredible eyes of his, his voice husky. "Hey, man, why didn't you say you want to do it again? I'm game if you are. Fuck, I've got butterflies just thinking about."

The atmosphere in the car was tight as a spring. Jason reached over to squeeze my cock. I realized I still had my hand on his crotch and pulled it away quickly.

"That was an accident," I stuttered.

"Man, you have the best accidents of anyone I know." He was attempting to pull down the fly on my trousers. I moved his hand.

"Jason, I…" I fudged it. "Jason, we can't do this again."

He was chipper in the face of my negativity. "Yes, we can. There's nothing stopping us."

"A father's sense of what's right and wrong is stopping us."

"We'll just have to rewire the old man's brain, get rid of those boring old societal constructs."

"Jason, I don't know what you're talking about but that has to be a one-off."

"Tell me you didn't like it. No. Tell me you didn't love it."

"I can't do that."

Jason was triumphant. "Because you did love it!"

"Of course, I did. What's not to love? You are one gorgeous young man. I was so hot for you."

"And I was sizzling for you," he admitted, and then mumbled. "Still am."

This was getting us nowhere. I chose to remain silent for the next few kilometers as I took my frustration out on the interstate trucks that clogged the road. I noticed he was pouting like the spoiled brat he once was, wondering what had changed him so. I ruffled his hair. It was the only fatherly thing I could think of to rouse him from his funk.

"Look, I know it's none of my business—"

"Then make it your business," he said.

"Are you always so…" I had to choose my words carefully, "…so brazen. So forward…"

"So slutty?" he added.

"If you like."

"Are you?"

I laughed. It broke the ice.

"Well?" He was persistent. "Are you?"

"That's not the sort of question a young guy asks his dad."

"This young guy does."

"Well this guy doesn't answer questions like that."

Jason leaned his knees against the dashboard. "Don't worry, dad. I'll worm it out of you. Or else, ask your mates."

I almost ran us off the road.

After I thought about it for a time, I told Cal, the name he preferred to go by, "You leave my friends totally alone."

He laughed. "You mean because they're all old enough to be my dad?"

"I'm serious," I warned.

"Or what? You'll spank me? Bring it on, old man."

I wasn't smiling when I said, "My friends are strictly off-limits."

He gave me a melodramatic pout and totally insincere hangdog look. "Yes, dad."

To Clive, I'd said, "Don't even think about it!"

"If he's as cute as you say, well a man's gotta do what a man's gotta do."

"What a man's gotta do is keep his cock in his pants around my son."

I guess I was hotter under the collar than I thought for he immediately backed off. "Hey, take it easy. I was only joking."

I didn't believe him. His hardening cock, clearly outlined in his gym shorts, gave the lie to what he said.

I was dreading the evening when Cal and I would have to confront the enormity of what we'd done. If there was an upside to the whole situation, it was that we'd overcome what had threatened to be an awkward initial meeting considering we'd parted six or seven years earlier loathing each other. There was no way to sustain that position after we'd fucked, unless...unless Cal blamed me for what had occurred.

I worried needlessly all afternoon. After my less-than-calming venting at Clive, I went back to the office, moody as fuck, and tore strips off anyone who came near me. Most of the workers gave me a wide berth until my secretary, Helen, came in with a coffee laced with rum and made me drink it all down, thus mellowing me out for what remained of the working day. I would have stayed at the office, I had plenty of important paper work to catch up on, but I knew I couldn't postpone the inevitable forever.

When I pulled into the driveway, the house was a blaze of lights and the CD was just loud enough that I could hear it as I approached the front door. I was expected because as I reached into my pocket to get my keys, the door opened and an arm thrust a relaxing scotch and dry at me. I had to smile. My secretary knows what I like. She'd obviously rung Cal to have him prepare an antidote. It broke the ice and I was smiling broadly as I entered.

Cal was not alone. Two young men lounged in the living room going through my collection of CDs, none of which my instinct said would interest them. I nodded in their direction.

"That's Derek and Izzy," Cal said. They looked up and nodded.

"Great collection of jazz CDs man," Izzy said. "You mind if I borrow some. This shit is rare."

"Help yourself, guys. Just one rule. You bring them back in the condition you found them or I'll cut your balls off." They glanced up, smiling, but they could tell I was serious. They mumbled their agreement to my terms.

"I met them at the uni as I was enrolling. They run the gay and lesbian campus group," Cal admitted. "I didn't think you'd mind if…"

"Just keep the noise down and don't get spunk on the rug," I said, relieved they were around Cal's own age, although if I was completely honest with myself, there was a twinge of jealousy somewhere in the pit of my stomach. I just wasn't sure whether I was jealous of Cal getting two personable young college studs who I would have given my right testicle to screw, or whether I was jealous that Izzy and Derek were likely to be plugging Cal's ass soon. I shook my head. I didn't want to go there.

"Da-ad," Cal groaned. "It's nothing like that."

I smirked. "If you say so. I'm just going up to change. You want takeaway for dinner or you want to go out?"

"Um, I hope you don't mind, but Izzy made some pasta and I was going to make a salad."

I pushed open the kitchen door to see water boiling on the stove and a deep red sauce bubbling beside it.

"I didn't know I had the ingredients," I admitted.

"You didn't," Izzy yelled from the living room, proving they were listening to every word. "We bought it on the way here. To repay the hospitality."

"In that case, I think it's my duty to supply the wine, don't you?"

"Cool," Izzy said.

As I made my way upstairs, I heard Derek say just loudly enough to carry so I expect he wanted me to hear, "Your dad is fuckin' hot. I'd let him do me."

"Over my dead body," Cal huffed.

"How about a foursome," Izzy suggested.

I chuckled as I entered my bedroom, out of earshot of their conversation, mentally noting to keep an eye on Derek and Izzy as possible future sexual partners. I must admit their admissions they found me desirable meant that I took more care with my shower and, particularly, my choice of clothes. Normally, I'd slouch around in shorts or track suit bottoms, this time I chose a pair of my tightest jeans that showed my bulge and my ass in their best light, plus I wore a T-shirt that hugged my pecs enough that my buds poked at the fabric. Cal raised a suspicious eyebrow when I came back downstairs as if to hint that he knew what my game was.

And it was just a game, after all.

The meal was simple, but delicious. "All we can afford as students. We live on dried noodles a lot," Izzy confided.

I turned my brightest smile on him. "We can fix that easily. How about you come over here for a bang up meal once a week."

Izzy blushed. "I'd really like that."

Derek wasn't about to be left out. "Me, too."

Cal's reaction was to kick me under the table. Hard.

In the end, Cal and I never had the 'big discussion.' Life moved on and neither of us seemed willing or interested in broaching the sensitive subject. Perhaps it was guilt, or fear, because we seemed to have developed a rapport that had never existed between us before, due in large part I suspect to our inadvertent coupling.

That's not to say sharing the same house with my son was easy. He had a tendency to flaunt his body, carelessly discarding clothes if it was too hot, too cold, too lukewarm, too anything in fact. He liked to swim naked in the backyard pool although I had to put my foot down and insist he wear his Speedos when we had guests, unless it was Derek and Izzy because then they'd all go skinny dipping and I could lie on the banana lounge, pretending to sleep while attempting to hide my excitement with my hand.

Occasionally one or both the boys would head off to the bedroom with Cal, or stay over, the sounds from the bedroom giving me blue balls. That's when I found it difficult, because I had put an unofficial ban on myself bringing home sex partners as long as Cal lived in the house. Fortunately, he was due to move into uni accommodation with his two new friends in a few short weeks.

My right hand was getting a regular workout. It was easy getting hard when I fantasized about Derek or Izzy except that Cal's image kept nuzzling them aside so that by the time I blew a load it was Cal who was foremost in my mind.

On one occasion I came home to find him in my bedroom watching my porn DVDs while porking his ass with one of my dildos. He didn't miss a beat when he saw me standing watching. "I can see why you keep these porn movies hidden in your closet, dad," he said. "They're super-hot. I got bored with that same old vanilla shit downstairs so I came searching. Glad I did. You're a man of singular tastes, dad. I like it."

"I see you like my toys as well."

"I knew you wouldn't mind."

I did mind but it seemed churlish to complain. "Make sure you wash them when you're finished."

"Don't go, dad. Come and help me out."

"I can't do that, Cal."

"Why?"

"You know why."

"I know you want to."

My cock, as usual, gave me away. I defy anyone to stand watching a hot college boy impaling himself on a seven-inch dildo, playing with his own cock and balls, and not get hard. I'd have to try harder to think like a father and not like a frustrated older man. Think of my boy as family and not a sex object. I found it hard to move my mind into another gear.

"Come on, dad. You fuckin' ignored me for the first twenty years of my life. You owe me."

Emotional blackmail. A nice touch. I was grasping at straws and, fragile as it was, I jumped at that justification. I sat on the bed. "Okay, but I'm just helping you out, there's none of that shit like we did at the airport–"

"Aw!"

"Then we talk."

"Aw, man. Way to ruin a guy's mood."

I shuffled to the head of the bed, still clothed although I was desperate to lie naked with him, Cal wriggling to lie against my chest so he could watch the movie. He'd chosen one of my favorites, a group of guys gangbanging a college stud during an initiation. Cal kept his eyes glued to the student having his ass stretched to accommodate eight huge cocks, "Lucky bastard."

"It's one of my favorites," I admitted.

"How would you like to watch it for real?"

"You and eight guys?"

His voice went all husky. "Yeah."

"Don't even go there. Fantasies are best left as fantasies."

I tweaked his nipples, pinching them hard, making him gasp at the pain.

"I like that," he whispered.

I grabbed his pecs, squeezing the muscle before pinching his nipples again then ran my hand across his hairless chest down to his belly. It was hard as marble. My fingers inched toward the prize, my breath heavy, and his caught in his throat in anticipation of what I might do next. I traced my fingers through his pubic hair, brushing against the shaft. He gulped, continuing to stare at the TV.

"Help me out, Buzz," he whispered. "I know you want to."

His voice was seductive, the porno was titillating, and my nerve endings were at screaming point. I ran the back of my hand along his shaft. My god, I wanted him so badly.

Tilting his head back, I could read desire in his eyes. He opened his mouth and I leaned forward to kiss him, his mouth upside down, his eyelashes dancing on my neck. The kiss was slow and sensual but full of desperate longing. It had been three weeks since our first encounter and I'd fought valiantly against repeating the experience but here I was surrendering. I couldn't help it.

I told myself I was just helping him out. I was still clothed although he would have felt my cock straining in my shorts. I broke the lip lock, desperate for oxygen. We were both panting.

"Fuck me, daddy," he pleaded.

I couldn't. I just couldn't. Much as my cock screamed that I wanted it. Instead, I put my hand on his and took control of the dildo plundering his butt hole and began to ram it home like I wanted so much to ram my cock inside his hot ass. I scooted down the bed to get better leverage while he, expecting that I was about to fuck him, opened his legs wider. He was so vulnerable and so goddam heart-stopping hot. I plunged the dildo in hard, twisting it as it lunged home, trying to find the spot inside that would send sparks through his body. It took a number of attempts but I did find it, reading my success in his face. Concentrating on that spot, I hesitated only slightly before I wrapped my hand around his weeping cock and began a smooth milking motion that would bring him off.

I heard the catch in his breath signifying he was close. "Do it, daddy," he whispered.

Synchronizing the thrusts into his ass and the downward stroke on his cock, I sped up until he was writhing under my touch. Loud panting filled the room, as much me as him, then I felt the pulse in his dick as the cum surged up his shaft to splatter all over my hand and his stomach while I kept the dildo embedded totally inside his ass.

"Oh, fuck," he screamed, repeating it over and over until he collapsed on the bed. I got up to leave after a suitable intermission, mainly to clean up because I had blown a load in my pants, but he grabbed my hand, pulling me back. "Don't go. Stay with me."

I wanted so much to reject the invitation, to draw a line under what had just occurred, but, in the end, I capitulated to my own need. I drew his body against mine and cuddled him as he fell asleep.

I dozed intermittently, gazing at my handsome companion's face as he drooled over my chest, his breath coming in relaxed waves, wondering where my son had gone. What alien had taken over the body and mind of the overweight homophobic asshole that I had last seen? Who was responsible for the personality transplant? And did his surgery have a side specialty in the removal of guilt glands? Sign me up please!

Cal stirred about an hour later, rubbing his hands across the crusted cum on his body. "Time for a shower, I think," he said without a hint of recrimination to his voice. "Want to join me, old man? We can take this to the next level."

My body screamed 'yes' but my mouth said, "I think I'd better get us something to eat."

He didn't argue. "Chicken," he tossed at me as he headed to the bathroom, dropping his towel so he had to bend forward to pick it up and in so doing give me an eyeful of his delectable ass. "See something you like?" he added as he straightened up and flounced into the shower. "I never lock my bathroom door."

It would have been so easy just to walk in and fuck him against the cold tiles, but I was never one for the easy solution. Instead, I went to the kitchen to prepare the evening meal while guzzling sufficient vodka that by the time Cal emerged, I was feeling no pain.

My silence stilled his usual chattering and the meal was a forlorn affair until Cal put down his fork and sighed. "Look, dad. I'm sorry I went into your bedroom and searched through your shit. I shouldn't have done it, okay?"

"No 'Sorry I talked you into getting me off'?"

He replied with that smile of his. No one could resist that.

"But that porno was so hot, right? Those DVDs must be your favorites to have them stashed in your bedroom. You into gangbangs, man?"

"Are you?"

"Have you noticed how you don't answer any direct questions of a personal nature?"

"Have you noticed that in the great big world outside your head kids don't ask their parents intimate questions about their sex lives?" I responded.

"Maybe they should," he said simply. "Perhaps what families need is greater honesty."

I raised an eyebrow. "Really?"

"Yeah. Ask me anything. Anything at all."

I was game. "Okay…"

"But I expect the same in return."

My next 'okay' was a little less sure.

I went first. I tried to keep it light, non-confrontational. "What have you done with Jason? How much will it cost to get him back?"

Cal laughed. "You don't really want him back." Then his face clouded. "Do you?"

"Actually, I was thinking of paying you to keep him away longer."

"No payment necessary." Cal took a deep breath. "I was an asshole, dad. What can I say? I was a deeply unhappy kid. When puberty hit I was confused. I couldn't go to dad, my step-dad I mean. He and mum are fundamentalists when it comes to morality. Don't touch. Don't kiss. Don't hug. Deal with it. I didn't have anyone to turn to."

Sorry," I mumbled.

"Not your fault. I grew up in a household where 'faggot' was the worst name you could call someone. Then I started getting…feelings. I couldn't discuss it with them. So I asked if I could come see you. That was when I was fourteen going on fifteen. I had this idealized picture in my mind that you would embrace me, we could talk things over man to man, but something got in the way."

"Maybe if I'd tried harder."

"No, that's not it," he smiled. "I liked you. I liked everything about you. The honesty in the way you lived. Your friends. Everything. But, most of all, I liked you. A little bit too much."

I think the stunned look on my face said everything I had no words for.

"Yeah. I was turned on by the man who was my dad. You treated me with respect and I repaid you by being the biggest asshole in the history of the universe. I didn't know how else to behave. I knew I was turning you away from me. I couldn't deal with it. I'm sorry, dad. When I went back home, I was so moody they thought something must have happened. It did, but not what they thought. When you didn't keep in touch I was hurt. I understood, but I was hurt. After I got over it, I went out and got myself a life. I was a rebellious bastard. Mum and step-dad wiped their hands of me, almost threw me out. But I settled down. That's when I hatched the plan to come back here and make it up to you."

Heat scorched across my face. "I don't need a pity fuck!"

"Oh, for Christ's sake, listen to yourself," he shouted. "This is not about fucking. I didn't know who you were at the airport, I swear it. I thought you were one hot fucker. Still do. And I think you still fancy me, too. Don't you?"

I went to deny it.

"Honesty. Remember?"

"God help me, yeah, I think you're the hottest little fucker I've ever seen. There. Satisfied?"

"I'd be much more satisfied if you'd throw me on the table and fuck me." He saw the look on my face. "But you won't?"

I shook my head. My heart bucked like a steam hammer in my chest.

"No matter, old man. I can wait. I have youth on my side." He slapped my ass as he sashayed provocatively to the sink with his plate.

The game was on.

Life with Cal settled down to good-natured parry and thrust, although I dexterously evaded his every request that I lunge myself inside him. I don't think either of us took it seriously although my cock ached every time he flaunted his body at me. The nights he had a 'friend' stay over were delicious agony. I would jerk off to the sounds in the room next door or if guilt over-rode my lust, I would take myself for a long walk through the neighborhood until I knew they'd be asleep.

The time was rapidly approaching when he would move out to be closer to the university when the new semester began. His twenty-first birthday also loomed. I thought he'd want to fly back to be with the folks who brought him up. I was happy to pay his fare knowing that they were not wealthy. I'd organize a party on his return. He surprised me by saying, "It's no big deal, dad. I'd prefer to stay here if it's all the same to you." I had the uneasy feeling there was something he was not telling me. It could wait.

I discussed Cal's birthday party and his present at length with Clive. I have no idea what a young man wants. Not strictly true, of course, but I wanted it to be a special occasion for him. The party would not be a large affair, just my close friends, the people he'd insulted on his previous visit, plus the new friends he'd made at university. I knew the few women who would be in attendance would leave early in the evening, the straight men would hang around until the atmosphere became just that little bit too libidinous.

Not that there was anything even remotely sexual planned for the evening. I suspected Cal would disappear at some stage with Derek and Izzy, both of whom I'd come to like immensely over the few weeks in which I'd known them. They were level-headed young men with just enough curiosity about sex and recreational substances not to abuse either. They'd be great eye candy for the men of my age who would predominate at the party.

My friends had all called around to see the prodigal; too many of them had to force their tongues back in their mouths for fear of slobbering over him for my liking. Cal seemed more amused by the reaction he got than disgusted or displeased. I suppose it stroked his ego although they were definitely keen to stroke something else if they could just get their hands on it.

The day before the big event, he received a letter from his mum and her husband. He'd been rather close-fisted regarding his contact with them and I didn't pry. He took the letter to his bedroom to read, returning half an hour later with tears in his eyes. From laughing. He was still cracking up as he tossed an envelope on the table.

"Just what every boy needs for his birthday," he laughed.

I didn't want him making fun of his family, and I didn't want him making a big deal out of my gift either. "Look, I know money is in short supply back home."

"It's not that, dad. It's not the cost; it's the thought that goes into it. It says a lot about how a person feels about you."

I picked up the envelope he obviously meant me to open while he rubbed himself against me. He was teasing. "So what did you get me, dad? A rubber facsimile of your cock cause you won't give me the real thing?"

"In your dreams." I laughed out loud when I saw his gift: a one hundred dollar voucher. In itself, that was a fair enough gift. The sting was in its redemption. It could only be used at a certain Christian bookshop.

"Well, there's one hundred dollars' worth of goods that will go unclaimed," he said. I was pleased that he wasn't ungrateful, merely amused.

He didn't pester me about whether I'd bought him anything, he seemed content just to be spending time with me, so when I presented him with an envelope the next morning at breakfast, he was genuinely surprised.

"Please tell me this is not a two hundred dollar voucher at a Christian bookshop, unless they sell dildos."

"Damn," I said. "You guessed."

His mouth gaped. "Fuck, dad. Tell me this is not what I think it is."

"It's out the front," I told him.

He was up from the table and out the door before I even finished the sentence. By the time I caught up, he was doing a jig on the footpath trying to open the car door and failing miserably in his excitement.

Taking the key from him, I unlocked the doors with the remote. The car was second-hand and nothing special but it was all his. It gave him independence. He hugged me as he took back the keys, his eyes misty, but not enough that he didn't take the opportunity to grope me.

He whispered into my ear. "Don't believe for a minute, old man, that I misinterpret this. I understand the significance. You're not trying to buy me off for not being around when I grew up. This is your way of saying you still want me around when I move out and that I have no excuse for not coming over."

Pecking me on the lips, he went to the driver's door, hesitating before he climbed in. "You coming?"

"Thanks, but I've got a party to organize or have you forgotten? Besides, you, Derek and Izzy don't need me cramping your style while you're hooning around."

"As if," he said, adding more sincerely. "Thanks dad. For everything."

He was gone in a screech of tyres and a fart of exhaust on his way to adulthood, if such a hoary old concept still existed. I marveled that he was so much more mature at this age than I ever had been. Back then, I'd been married and fathered a child. The one that just took off down the road. God, I felt old.

The party itself turned out to be a good combination of young and older, gay and straight, although men outnumbered women five-to-one. Cal was gregarious, equally at home with all the partygoers, spending time with my heavily pregnant secretary Helen although I think they spent most of the time talking about me as they were always glancing surreptitiously in my direction. She'd come with her husband Phil, a borderline homophobe who remained at the party after he'd packed his wife off home early with other departing guests. I remembered Helen said he liked his booze, especially if it's free, and alcohol was flowing like water at this celebration.

Clive volunteered to attend the bar, although Phil took it upon himself to act as relief on many an occasion. Both were free with the nips of spirits and stingy with the mixer. I wasn't too concerned as it's not every day your only son turns twenty-one. As the night progressed, I was feeling very light-headed. I hoped Cal was taking it easy.

He seemed popular, many of the men lined up to dance with him, and I couldn't help but feel pride when I saw what a fine young man he'd grown into, the antithesis of what he'd been at fourteen.

The food was catered. Smorgasbord, nothing elaborate, but enough to soak up the alcohol without being too cheap or too classy. As Baby Bear would say, 'Just right.' It even impressed Izzy who tracked me down to thank me for catering to his dietary needs: he's vegan. "Not many people take any notice when I tell them, they think it's a joke or else too difficult. I appreciate it, Buzz." To show his appreciation he stuck his tongue down my throat and squeezed my cock which liked the feeling. I wasn't concerned about scaring the horses this late in the evening as the party poopers and early-to-bedders had departed after the food and the cutting of the cake, done sufficiently early that the serious partying could get underway sooner rather than later. When he came up for air, he looked me in the eye, "Of course, there is some sausage that I love to eat, and you have just the sort I like." Patting my hard-on, he flounced away, challenging me with "Think about it."

I glanced up to see Cal smiling from across the room. He strode over. "I hope that wasn't what it looked like."

"It probably was," I admitted. "He's had a bit too much to drink and was thanking me for making sure there was vegan food."

"If that's the sort of thanks you get for special catering imagine what I'd have to give you for a car. It'd take months, maybe years to pay it off. How about we begin tonight?"

"You don't want to spend such an important occasion with your old man. Go and have fun, just try not to let me catch you."

"You mean you'll be jealous?"

"I'm only flesh and blood," I said. My brain was telling me I'd had too much to drink and to shut my mouth now.

"I like the way your flesh and blood has been put together," he said, running his finger down the front of my jeans. "You make me hot."

"Not gonna happen."

"I thought you wanted this birthday to be special."

"Don't try blackmail, Cal. Not tonight."

"You've got quite a few hot friends who might like to make the night special, even if you don't."

"Don't even go there. These men are my close friends."

He just laughed as he walked off, giving me the finger good-naturedly. Then why did I have a sinking sensation in the pit of my stomach? Some gnawing feeling told me I couldn't let him walk off like that. I tapped the side of my glass. "Attention everyone. Everyone." The babble subsided. Someone turned the music down.

I hadn't prepared anything but I launched into it anyway, speaking blindly but probably more truthfully as a result. "Thanks for coming this evening. I see the usual suspects have lingered long after most people have turned into pumpkins." My friends laughed. "And thanks to Cal's friends from university, it's good to see you here tonight. Most of you know I had nothing to do with Cal's upbringing. His mum and his step-dad were responsible for the fine young man you see here before you today. I don't mind telling you I was far from pleased when I learned Cal was coming back here to attend university. Our last meeting had been anything but auspicious so my

48

expectations were at their lowest level. Imagine how very pleasantly surprised I was then to find the confident young man, the inquisitive young man, the handsome young man who is Cal today. I can honestly say I am so proud of what he has become, and…"

My eyes watered. Cal came over and put his arm around my shoulders.

"Before I make an even bigger fool of myself. Here's to Cal and his future happiness."

We all raised our glasses, and then someone yelled out 'speech' from the floor.

"Thanks dad. That goes double for me. What son wouldn't love to have such a hot man for a dad? I was a twat when I was here last time. I think I insulted, ridiculed or threatened most, if not all, you guys over thirty in this room, and for that I apologize unreservedly. But apologies are easy; it's our deeds we should be judged by. So, to make it up to my new friends, and I hope you're all that, and as my dad says, to further my future happiness, any of you who felt insulted or demeaned by my past behavior, I invite you to feel free to gangbang me or feel free to make use of my mouth in any way that makes you feel happy."

There was a shocked silence during which I saw monogamous gay couples discuss the offer before the young partygoers broke into a round of stomping and applause in appreciation. I used the cover of the uproar to grab Cal's elbow and steer him into a nearby room before closing the door.

"What do you think you're doing, Cal?"

"It's my party. It's my life."

"And it's my house. Is this because I won't fuck you again?"

"You figure it out, Einstein."

"You're pissed," I said.

"Big fuckin' deal."

"Pull yourself together while I go and dampen down the enthusiasm."

I left him sulking and went back into the party. No one had moved, waiting expectantly for the next scene.

"Sorry, guys, Cal's a bit emotional. Obviously, he was joking. It was the grog doing the talking—"

"Give him some more then," someone called out from the floor.

I avoided Cal for much of the rest of the night although I noticed he was even more popular than before. However, if anyone thought there was going to be a gangbang they would be sadly mistaken. That would occur only over my dead body, even if Cal looked as if he would like to arrange that.

Somewhere along the line I would have to apologize, I didn't want the day to end on a sour note. I noticed him duck upstairs alone. I was about to go after him when I got waylaid by a drunken Izzy who wanted to continue our earlier conversation. It took me a while to find Derek to offload him, then I hurried upstairs expecting to find Cal in the bathroom but it was empty. He must have gone to his bedroom so I headed down the hallway, my blood running cold when I heard him scream, "Fuck me harder, you bastard. Give it all you've got."

A string of profanities that would make a sailor turn teetotal followed as I made my way toward the sound, heart in my boots. Cal was facing the open door, wild eyed so that at first I didn't think he recognized me, his mouth spewing out his desire for the most grotesque humiliation and degradation. Phil was pounding his ass, red in the face from attempting to satisfy Cal's craving for total submission.

Phil called out to me, "For God's sake stuff something in his mouth to get him to shut up. He's like a wild animal. He's fuckin' insatiable."

My cock was hard the moment it saw Cal on the receiving end of straight cock, taking it like a slut. But if my cock was excited, my mind wanted to flee. I started to close the door in case anyone else stumbled across the scene.

"Leave the fuckin' door open, old man," Cal snarled. "You may not want to fill my mouth but there are plenty of others who will."

I walked away; I couldn't bear to watch any more. I went to my bedroom, shutting the door against the banshee curses and foul demands. Was this my fault? Was this as a result of the pick-up at the airport? I blamed myself because there was no one else. I cursed myself for being so weak. If I'd given him what he wanted, would he be the sex-starved animal I'd seen in the bedroom? If I'd been more of a man would I have pulled Phil off my son and thrown him down the stairs? What did it matter? I'd done neither.

My door burst open, interrupting my guilt, and Cal stood naked in the light. He staggered over to the bed before I could sit up, throwing himself down on top of me. He ground his mouth against mine and I tasted spunk. Someone had taken him up on the offer of a blow job. He was like a man possessed as he ground his body against me, attempting to unbuckle my trousers as he shoved his tongue as far into my mouth as he could. He pulled my hair to keep my head still, licking my lips and my nose, showering my eyelids with kisses and biting my neck before again kissing me with his sperm-slicked tongue.

"I want you, Buzz. And I'm gonna have you," he whispered savagely as he turned to face the base of the bed in order to get my trousers down. I had gone commando again so I was soon naked from the waist down. In kneeling down to take my cock in his mouth, he pushed his ass against my face.

"Eat my ass, Buzz."

I parted his cheeks with my hands and pushed my face toward his musky hole, my tongue swiping the entrance to his guts. It was moist because Phil had his cock embedded there moments earlier. The idea of eating Phil's spunk made my cock harder.

"Taste good, daddy? You like your little boy's ass, ripe with another man's hot jizz?"

I mumbled as he squashed his butthole against my face so I could scarcely breathe then squeezed it open so

I tasted not one but many men's loads fermenting inside him.

"You taste them all, daddy. All the men who want me. Not weak men like you. They know what they want and they take it. Eat their spunk, daddy. Get some ball juice; grow a pair of your own."

The cum puddled out of his ass, sliming my mouth and chin as I tried to suck it all up.

"You like that? I knew you would. Well, I got another surprise for you tonight, daddy."

I was still reeling from lack of oxygen so it scarcely registered when Cal pushed my legs into the air, swiped my asshole with two fingers of lube, positioned his cock at the entrance, and pushed.

"Holy fuck," I screamed.

The entire neighborhood must have heard my pain.

Cal didn't let up. He attacked my ass with the ferocity of a tiger but, once the pain had subsided, I matched him, mashing my mouth against his, pushing my ass back against his belly until he had every inch inside me, pummeling me into the mattress. The pain was good. He spewed his abuse verbally and physically, pounding me until I thought every bone in my body would ache the next day. It would all climax in Cal spewing his cum and his contempt up my ass.

I had never felt so alive, felt such passion, such animal desire. I wanted him to rip into my ass. "Fuck me, son," I shouted. I matched him stroke for stroke, thrust for thrust, and curse for curse until nothing and no one existed outside our frenzied coupling. I was so turned on I felt invincible and I knew Cal felt the same way.

We would keep this up for hours; it was like some natural aphrodisiac. In the back of my mind, I knew there would be a price to pay but, fuck that, I'd worry about it in the morning.

SONNY & SHARED

*T*he day after Cal's birthday bash was the day from hell. I staggered out of bed with the first phone call, way too early to be anything but an emergency. My ass was sore from the unexpected pounding Cal had given it the previous night and I grimaced as I reached over to the bedside table to get the wretched electronic squaller.

I could barely open my eyes, although my befuddled brain did register that it was eight o'clock. I had to assume it was morning. Most god-fearing people were already at church, not a destination you'd find me.

My voice was croaky and spunk phlegmed. I had to clear it a number of times before I could get the word out. "Hello."

The responding voice was that of my sarcastic former wife, Irene. "Must have been some party."

I sighed loudly enough that she heard me. "What do you want, Irene? It's eight o'clock in the morning after a wild, uninhibited party."

"It's Sunday. I'm hoping Jason is at church."

"You hope in vain."

"I knew you'd corrupt him," she spat.

"Did you ever think he might corrupt me?"

There was a long pause. Obviously, that idea had not occurred to her.

"Is that possible?"

"All right, Irene, state your business and get off the phone."

"I want to speak to our son."

"I'll be more than happy to tell him you called, when he wakes up from his drunken and drug-fucked sleep. I'll even encourage him to ring you back to receive your birthday blessings, secular or religious as your heart dictates."

She was in the middle of shouting, "Don't you hang up on me," when I put the phone down. I'll give her credit. She didn't ring back.

That's more than can be said for some of the party guests from the debauchery of the night before.

I could not get back to sleep after Irene's call which had not awoken Cal who lay spread-eagled, naked on his back, in the bed beside me. While I gathered my wits, I took the time to really examine him. He was a magnificent piece of flesh and I felt a twinge that for all his proclamations of devotion, he could never be mine. Realistically he had his whole life ahead of him while mine was half over. I had made little of myself. Okay, I had a successful business which gave me a house and ample to live on. I was never overly ambitious. I did wonder whether I would have been more so for Cal's sake had I remained married.

It was no use going there. I went to the bathroom to piss away the booze and the 'might-have-beens,' as well as unload Cal's spunk from my ass. He'd fucked me hard and my ass was suffering this morning. Still, the face reflected blearily in the mirror was smiling. Shit! That was not a good sign.

I'd been so good fending off Cal's previous advances that I was unprepared for his sheer brutal dominance when he nailed me to the bed. We'd both given in to crazy sexual lusts after that, flip-flopping throughout the long night, Cal wild-eyed and insatiable, until we'd fallen asleep exhausted. My body warned me it needed more time to recover but my mind was so full of pornographic images it would not shut down. I took my body and my erection downstairs wrapped in a threadbare dressing gown I'd retrieved from the back of the wardrobe once Cal arrived to stay with me. I normally walked around naked when I lived alone.

"Don't change your behavior on my account, dad," Cal had smirked.

That was precisely why I had changed my style of living.

I put the coffee pod in the machine hoping the water was hot enough to make a decent cuppa. I didn't care really because I'd go for a second shortly to ease my aching head and my throbbing butthole. While I waited for the bloody machine to spit out my heart starter, I gathered up the bottles from the night before. The messy food plates, sticky with grease and part-digested snacks that had petrified during the night, could wait until my stomach settled down.

I'd finished clearing up the kitchen and was about to start on the living room, fortified by my second cup of strong coffee, when the front doorbell rang. It was Phil, my secretary's husband, looking sheepish but expectant.

"Great party," he whispered. "Enjoyed myself immensely."

I didn't like the guy much but his wife Helen was a hard-working savior to my business, and I was sorry to lose her to pregnancy. Slimy bastard Phil, whose mouth often ranted homophobic claptrap, took to my son's ass like the proverbial duck to water the previous night so I suspected ulterior motives for his early morning visit.

I was sarcastic. "Didn't get enough last night, Phil? Had to come back for a morning repeat, eh?"

His look of shock was so fake, it confirmed my suspicions.

"What are you talking about? What happened? I was so drunk I don't remember a thing after Helen went home."

"Yeah. I suspect there was a lot of memory loss last night. Anyway, why are you here?"

"Oh, I think I left my mobile phone. I just came over to see if I could find it because it has all my contact numbers on it. Have you seen it?"

I didn't believe a word. "Haven't been up all that long but I can tell you it's not in the kitchen. I don't mind if you want to look around."

"Thanks. I'd be lost without it."

"Why don't I ring it so you can track it down via its ring tone?"

"Ah, okay, but wait until I get upstairs, then give it a go. But I think the battery was low."

"Upstairs?"

"Yeah…uh…the last time I remember seeing it was when I went to the upstairs bathroom. Give me a few seconds then try."

"Okay."

He headed for the stairs. "Um, Cal around?"

"He's still sleeping it off. He was so pissed last night he didn't know what he was doing. Why?"

"Um, I don't think I wished him a happy birthday."

Phil's guilt was writ large on his flustered face and in everything he stuttered over.

"That's okay. I'll let him know when he wakes up."

"Thanks."

As the piece of human garbage headed off, I planned to dial his number, follow him up the stairs to ensure he left Cal alone, then shepherd him out of the house, but before I had an opportunity, the phone rang. It was Jake, one of my best mates with whom I'd shared a great many sleazy sex nights in the past. He'd never rung to thank me before so I knew immediately what his purpose was. He got around to it eventually.

"Cal has turned into one fine boy. You must be proud."

"Yeah, I am." I thought I'd make it easy for him because I wanted to get upstairs. "Except for that comment about, you know…"

"What?"

"Damn it, Jake. That silly nonsense about sleeping with all you guys to make up for insulting you."

"Oh, that. So, he wasn't serious?" He must have realized what he said implicated his motives. "I mean, I didn't take him seriously but I think some of the other guys might have. Um, is he around? I just want to wish him a happy birthday and tell him there are no…um…hard feelings on my side."

I almost laughed out loud. What a wanker. "No, Jake, he's still sleeping it off. Far too much to drink for a young kid, but he'll get over it."

"Uh, okay. I might call round later and wish him the best."

"Make it late because I think he'll be feeling a lot of pain when he wakes up."

No sooner had I sighed at the perfidy of some of my friends than the phone rang again. It was Zach, the dolly boy lover of Artie, the muscle mountain of a body who looked after the guys in the company warehouse.

"Great party, Buzz," he chirped. All my friends had picked up the habit of calling me Buzz since Cal had blown into town. I liked it so I made no objections.

"Yeah, Cal had a good time," I said non-committally.

He snickered. "I'll bet, especially after that suggestion he'd take on all the guys he'd insulted in the past. If he did that his ass would be run ragged for weeks."

I wasn't going to help out this time because I'd heard rumors about his relationship. Seems Zach was your typical snitty queen with a vicious tongue who loved to show off his muscle boyfriend's prowess by hiring him out for stud duties at rage parties and private poker nights. I didn't trust him.

When I said nothing, Zach decided discretion was the best tack. "Um, any guys at the party take him up on it?"

I decided on a lie this time. "I doubt it. I don't think any of my friends would be that disloyal to me they'd fuck my son, do you?"

He stumbled over himself to agree. "Of course not."

"Besides, he wasn't serious."

"Wasn't he?"

I could hear the disbelief in Zach's voice. "That's all right then. Though I wouldn't trust some of the people at the party, they were openly boasting…"

"Boasting what, Zach?"

"Never mind, it was obviously all a lie. You know how people are at parties."

At least he didn't ask to speak to Cal. He'd have to find another route to my son.

Next, I fielded a call from Helen who was looking for Phil. We exchanged a few pleasantries during which I told her Phil was upstairs looking for his phone.

"Oh, I swear that man loves his booze so much he must still be hung over. I heard him using it this morning to talk to Jake. They were planning some sort of ride with Cal for his birthday."

"He'll enjoy that." The problem was I thought he really would. "I'll get Phil to call you straight back."

I bounded up the stairs and along the corridor. If I hadn't known exactly where I'd find him, his loud ravings about 'hot faggot ass' and 'fuck you until you can't stand up' would have been better than a GPS navigation unit.

Bursting into my bedroom, I dragged Phil, trousers and boxers around his ankles, off the comatose Cal. Phil's cock slurped, spewing spunk across Cal's butt cheeks, as it broke free of his ass.

"Get out!" I screamed, scarcely containing my anger.

Phil scrambled to pull up his clothes, stumbling as he made for the door.

"You sick bastard! He's not even conscious."

Rather than back down, Phil sneered, getting a real ugly look on his face. "Fuck you! The kid loves it. Can't get enough. You've got a real slut on your hands. If you think you can control him, or tell your mates to lay off, you're fuckin' dreaming."

"I could always inform Helen," I threatened.

"And watch her lose the baby? Anyway, it's your word against mine. I'll tell her your slutboy came on to me while I was drunk. She'll believe me because she doesn't want to bring up a kid on her own. Checkmate."

I followed him down the stairs barely controlling the urge to kick his butt. As he reached the door, he turned on me. "You can't watch his back twenty-four/seven. There are a lot of guys out there just waiting for you to turn your back to slip your kid a hot poker between his ass cheeks. Mark my words."

After he left, I leaned against the door and sighed.

A voice interrupted my thoughts. "He's right you know."

It was Izzy.

"Yeah, I do know."

"He's not a total slut. He did it to make you jealous."

"I know."

"For someone who knows so much, you're remarkably stupid."

I couldn't take offence because I agreed with him, so I laughed.

"Come on, I'll make you breakfast and give you that birds and bees talk except it's all about bees and bees."

The smell of bacon sizzling attracted Derek and he soon joined us in the kitchen for the party debrief. They'd stayed overnight in the spare room, both of the opinion that once Cal had dorm accommodation at the uni he'd calm down. It was the close proximity to me that brought out the 'worst' in him. I put worst in parentheses because I knew a lot of men who thought I should be writing best.

We'd attempted to rouse Cal for breakfast but he merely groaned in pain and rolled over in bed. We force fed him some aspirin for the mammoth headache he was likely to suffer, and let him be.

During our explicit conversation about the previous night's events, the phone rang a number of times, the callers all offering profuse thanks for a wonderful evening and finishing by asking to speak to Cal. His young friends I passed on to Derek to respond, my friends I fielded myself. I wanted to know which of them I could trust. I was greatly annoyed when Clive rang. At least he was forthright about his intentions, coming right to the point.

"That fuckable little boy of yours up and about yet, Buzz?" he asked as if that sort of reference to my son was acceptable morning conversation. When I told him Cal was still sleeping it off, he added, "Look, let him know I rang and to pencil me into one of the time's he's available to take my cock up that delectable ass of his."

I shocked him with my reply. "If you think I'm going to let you fuck my son, you're deluded."

"It's got nothing to do with you who he fucks," Clive laughed down the phone, irritating me even more. "He's his own man. He can fuck who he likes."

"Not while he lives with me," I replied.

"Hey, man, I hope we're not gonna fall out over a fuck."

"That's entirely up to you."

I hung up before he could annoy me any further. I saw Izzy and Derek exchange worried looks. They also stole glances at my crotch. I was not aware my dressing gown had come adrift and my cock was on open display. Fuck! It was hard and oozing pre-cum. I had to believe it was having two cute twinks in their underwear seated at the table with me rather than the idea of Clive and my other friends fucking my little boy.

Derek got up and began massaging my shoulders and neck. "Man, you are so tense. You'd snap if you were a twig."

I relaxed into his soothing touch, closing my eyes, wondering if my life would have been simpler if Cal had not come to stay. My whole body tingled, especially my cock. I suddenly realized it felt that way because someone had his mouth around it. I looked down through the glass kitchen table to watch Izzy sucking the tension out of me via my dick. These two guys were better than aromatherapy and NLP therapy combined.

A perky voice interrupted us. "Can anyone join the party?"

It was a natural reflex to try to cover up but Derek held me firm in the seat and Izzy wasn't about to let go of my dick. I couldn't believe after all the heavy drinking and even heavier sex plus, I suspected, a little recreational drug use, Cal could be so bright and breezy. There was no justice in the world.

"The more the merrier," Derek smiled.

"I don't think this is a good idea," I said sharply as I struggled to get up.

Cal disagreed, crawling on all fours to take his place beside Izzy between my legs. "Oh, I do," he said. "Move aside, amateur. Let me show you how it's done."

Izzy did as he was told but not without a flare of aggravation. I struggled again, attempting to push Cal away with my foot without success.

"You might as well relax and enjoy it," Derek said, squeezing my muscles harder.

The moment Cal licked my cock head before wrapping his lips around the shaft, I knew the struggle was over. Somehow, Izzy had twisted his body under the chair and was licking at my balls. I shuffled forward to give him better access, longing to close my eyes to really appreciate the feeling but they remained fixed on my gorgeous twink son swallowing my cock like a professional.

I didn't want to believe what everyone said about him, but the proof was right in front of me, and it was hard to deny. Well, maybe he wasn't a total slut; he hadn't fucked everyone at the party, as far as I knew. But then, what did I know? Cal's formative years were a closed book to me. Perhaps there was something in his past...

My thoughts were brought back to the present sharply when Cal bit down on my shaft. He must have noticed my mind wandering and wanted my undivided attention. Call me perverse, but there's no finer sight than your own son chowing down on your meat, and he was doing an admirable job.

I told myself to make the most of it as this would be the last time. Cal and I would go our separate ways once he began his studies and I'd only see him when he deigned to visit which, if I knew young men, would become less and less frequent until it was only my birthday, if that.

Meanwhile, I concentrated on the spreading warmth in my dick and my balls, holding off for as long as I could before I shot a huge load of jizz down my boy's eager throat. Fuck, it was good! I collapsed into the chair, wrung out and satisfied, albeit somewhat disgusted by what had happened. I use the word 'somewhat' because the feeling was so good, so perverse, that I could never totally distance myself from it.

Cal got up, smacking his lips. "Okay, that was starters. What's for breakfast?"

Knowing they wouldn't discuss the personal stuff in front of me, I withdrew to take a shower, pausing at the top of the stairs until I saw Cal open the kitchen door to ensure I wasn't eavesdropping. On his return to the kitchen, I crept down the stairs to take up my possie within hearing distance of the kitchen conversation. By the time I tuned in, Izzy and Derek were berating Cal about his behavior.

"You can't keep treating your dad like that," Izzy said.

Cal acted innocent. "Like what?"

"Trying to make him jealous by fucking all his best friends. That's just weird," Derek remonstrated.

"I'm not trying to fuck all his friends," Cal said indignantly.

"Well, you made a bloody good fist of it last night," Izzy said.

"What!"

Derek explained. "After your dad's speech, you got up and told everyone that to make amends for the way you'd treated them in the past, they could all fuck you."

Cal groaned. "God, I must have been drunk. I don't remember that. So how many did I do?"

I heard the sizzle of more bacon as Izzy replied. "We didn't keep count but it couldn't have been all that many because after you let that disgusting Phil guy seed your ass—"

"I what?"

"That guy boasted to the whole party that he'd nailed you so good you were begging for a repeat. Not only that, he came back this morning pretending he'd left his phone here and fucked you while you were unconscious. Only the fact your dad pulled him off you and threw the bastard out, he'd probably still be inside you."

"All I remember is I fucked Buzz. Bloody good it was, too. I fucked him because he wouldn't fuck me."

"Did you ever think," Derek said patiently, "The reason he doesn't want to fuck you is that he doesn't want to stick his dick where all his friends have been? That wouldn't exactly make him seem special."

"By the way," Izzy interrupted. "There have been at least half a dozen calls this morning from men who want to poke your ass, and that's leaving aside the ones from guys at uni. Your dad doesn't seem jealous of them."

"Dad's jealous?"

"Well d'uh," Derek said. "Isn't that the intention? And incidentally, he's threatened to cut off all contact with his best mate, Clive, if he fucks you. Clive, I might add, is so keen he doesn't care if he loses your dad's friendship."

Cal groaned. "What have I done? All I wanted was for my dad to be my fuck buddy."

"Yeah, um…" Izzy began. "I'm not exactly sure that that's considered normal behavior. But having seen your dad, it's perfectly understandable, particularly as you haven't seen each other in eight years or so. Still…"

"What am I gonna do about all this guys?"

"Do you want to fuck them?" Izzy asked.

"A few of them are cute."

"I gather," Izzy said, "That they've been ringing each other so I'm guessing it's you do one you do 'em all, or shit will hit the fan."

"And just precisely how do I do that? Have a conga line of horny men coming to the door?"

"Leave it to Izzy, he always has a plan," Derek said.

"It just so happens that I do. I could see only one way out of this. You're a bit of a slut–"

"Hey."

"It wasn't a moral judgment, merely a statement of fact. I love sluts. One of my best friends is a slut."

"Okay, then."

"None of the guys is exactly ugly, though at least one of them has the personality of a rattlesnake…"

"Let me guess," said Cal. "You mean Zach?"

Izzy nodded. "But, he won't be fucking you with his personality."

"True."

"And that muscle-bound boyfriend of his is freakin' gorgeous."

"You always did look on the bright side, Izzy," Derek said.

"So, you're saying I should fuck them all?"

"Yep." Izzy sounded proud of his plan. "You tell them it's a one-time thing to make amends and that they should keep it to themselves unless they want to lose Buzz's friendship."

"Excuse me for pointing out a flaw to your plan, Izzy," Derek said, "But a steady stream of mid-aged men into a uni dorm is bound to attract unwanted attention."

"That's why Cal has to do it while he's living at home."

"Buzz will be so pleased," Cal said sarcastically.

Izzy was indignant. "No, give me credit. First, you pull a train."

Derek was incensed. "Do 'em one after the other?"

I could hear the smile in Cal's voice. "Mmm, that does have its appeal."

"Yeah, I thought it might."

"I may need the help of some recreational substances, but nothing that takes away the pleasure, or the memory."

"Or the pain, I expect," Derek added.

"So tell me why a line of men outside my bedroom door will go down better with Buzz than the same number spread out over a longer period."

"Because he won't know about it. That's the big plus of this plan. You told us your dad goes away on business every few weeks and stays away overnight. He usually knows a week or so in advance so you send out a general invite to the men involved, tell them it's a one-shot and there are no rain checks. Come one, come all, and don't expect to come again."

"The spare room won't fit all the guys who are likely to turn up," Derek said.

"And I don't want to use dad's room," Cal said.

Izzy had it all mapped out. "Two choices then. The living room. That way guys can watch the action or porn on the telly while they wait. Or if it's a warm enough evening, outside by the pool."

"What are you guys gonna be doing during all this?"

"We'll cater. Drinks and pizzas or something like that. Keep the lube warm and in fresh supply. Generally make sure it doesn't get out of hand."

Cal chuckled. "Maybe I could charge them if they're that keen. It would pay my fees for a few months at least."

As plans go, it was not a bad one, although I didn't want to know my boy was fucking all my best friends. Perhaps though, it was a great way to test their loyalty. I'd let it be known that I would not appreciate any sexual overtures to my son as a result of his open invitation at the party. I'd wangle a list of names out of Izzy of those who turned up. I was pretty sure I could bribe the list out of him by offering up my dick.

The remainder of the weekend passed uneventfully although the calls kept coming. I knew there was only one way to stop them once and for all. Sunday night while the four of us were having a makeshift meal, prepared by Izzy whose cooking I was getting to like a little too much, I orchestrated a phone call. Everyone tensed as they had throughout the day in case it was another proposition for Cal. I glanced at the caller ID.

"It's a work call. Sorry, guys, I've gotta take this. It's from one of our suppliers out of town."

I stood just on the other side of the kitchen door so they could hear every word of mine. I'd asked a guy I know to ring at the set time, wait for me to answer and then hang up, I'd take care of the rest of it. He thought he was getting me out of a boring dinner party and I wasn't about to tell him otherwise.

"Yeah, Pete, that sounds good for me but what about the other components that you promised?" I'd rehearsed the call in my head during the day to make it sound feasible, right down to the pauses. "But I gotta have those components otherwise your shit will be sitting around while I wait. (pause) Okay, but I'll be losing money on the deal. (pause) Why can't Frank handle that? (pause) Look at it from my point of view and it makes sense. I know it's extra effort but in this financial climate… (pause, with added sigh) All right, I'll tell you what I'll do. It's bloody inconvenient but what the fuck, it'll save money in the long term. I'll drive up on Saturday afternoon, drop into the factory, see if I can sort something out with Frank, then drop over to see you with the results of our meeting, and we can do a phone hook-up to sort out the whole mess. I can be back here late

Sunday afternoon. Sound feasible? (pause) Good man. See you Saturday night. I'll be at the usual hotel. (pause) Yeah, the one on Mann and Gosford Rd."

I heard whispering in the kitchen after I'd hung up from my phantom call, so I gave them time to make hurried arrangements before cursing and slamming back to the table as if pissed off. I couldn't miss the smirk of satisfaction on Izzy's face as he looked at his two confederates. I hoped I was doing the right thing.

"Trouble at factory, Buzz," Izzy asked putting on a northern English accent.

"Aye, lad." That was about as much as I could imitate. I made up some crap about how I'd need to leave around lunch-time Saturday but I'd be back in the afternoon the following day. I cursed my luck, telling Cal I would have liked to spend more time with him.

The three of them commiserated with me sincerely enough that I would have believed them if I didn't know better. Izzy from that moment intercepted all the incoming calls. "Let me, Buzz. I know they're aggravating. I know how to handle them so they won't call back."

Indeed he did. Each call that was for Cal's services he took in another room obviously whispering about the Saturday night free-for-all. It perturbed me that I didn't know how many accepted the invitation because surely some of them turned it down if only on the grounds that it was a gangbang. What perturbed me greater was the fact my cock got hard every time the phone rang and Izzy left the room.

It was a long week but real problems at work kept me occupied so I wasn't thinking of the forthcoming 'nuptials' in any great depth. I'd worked out my plan of action before I faked the call. I had no intention of actually being out of the house during the party. I intended nailing every bastard who turned up. While Cal was out, I had a mate set up a camera hidden high in the wall of the living room, camouflaged by the garish wallpaper I'd never replaced after Irene left. I also had one installed overlooking the pool area. That one was much easier to disguise. An added difficulty was that I wanted sound to go with the picture. I paid a small fortune for that, even though it wasn't perfect.

The pictures and sound fed straight into a computer I'd set up in the shed at the back of the pool area. I'd also stored supplies for my lengthy stay. Enough to get me through. Yeah, I felt like a pervert but what else is new?

On Saturday around lunch-time, three very jittery young men who were dancing about as if standing on hot coals, waved me off in the car. Instructing them to be good and, if they had a party, not to be too noisy, they looked embarrassed but I smiled reassuringly and they relaxed. I wasn't sure that the slap of cock against ass cheek or the slurp of dick entering mouth would be loud enough to disturb the neighbors from our enclosed pool area. They would not be able to see anything unless they peaked through the back fence.

My plan was simple: I would drive the car to a twenty-four hour car park, cab it back to within a few blocks of home, creep through the back, and ensconce myself in the shed. I had to time it impeccably so that no one was about. I knew Izzy and Derek would be out getting extra lube and other party accessories so I waited near the back fence until I heard the shower in Clay's room and his slightly off-key rendition of a current pop favorite. It made me smile that my son seemed so unconcerned about what was about to happen. It also made my cock super hard.

It had turned out a beautiful, hot day so I knew the party would get under way around the pool which was to my advantage as I could watch most of the action live rather than by webcam which I would have to rely on once it moved to the living room. Only the pool and the kitchen were close enough for me to watch via the peepholes I had drilled in the walls.

I had checked and double-checked everything I needed so it was just a matter of waiting, although my cock kept insisting it needed immediate attention. No way. I was buzzed by the anticipation. In fact, my whole body tingled at the thought of what I was going to witness. Somewhere during the week, this gangbang had gone from being a total betrayal by my friends to a rather ball-busting live action full-throttle gang fuck of the son who turned me on like the lights at an amusement park, but I didn't have the guts to fuck him into the ground myself, except when caught unawares.

But even anticipatory tumescence palls eventually and the long wait became tedious. I lay back in my comfortable chair and fell asleep. It was the sound of men cavorting in the pool that awoke me. I quickly peeked through my spy holes. A number of people were milling about, one or two already in the pool. If I hadn't known better, it looked just like an ordinary barbecue or pool party. The guys were dressed casually, chatting among themselves, although there was a palpable sense of sexual energy in the air.

I powered up the computer and checked the living room. They'd moved the furniture back so that there was a large central area, the coffee table taking pride of place like a sacrificial altar in the middle of the room. The floor was covered by a large plastic sheet. I almost blew in my shorts when I saw that. This was serious sexual shit.

Over the next half hour or so the party swelled to about fifteen or sixteen men, all seeming friends or acquaintances of mine. I noticed Clive and Phil were significantly absent, and that Zach was rallying the troops handing out little blue pills, obviously hoping to extend the men's staying power. The bastard had never liked me, convinced I was over-working and under-paying his boyfriend, Artie. Getting my best friends to fuck my son would be the ultimate humiliation in his eyes. I didn't rule out the possibility that he intended letting the secret out at some appropriate juncture with the potential to embarrass me. At the very least, he must have hoped it would drive a wedge between me and Artie so he'd be forced to look for another, hopefully better paid, position.

I wished I'd had enough foresight to prep myself with cock hardening goodies as well. Mine was going to need constant attention over the next twenty-four hours. Earlier, I noticed, via the webcam, that Cal had also resorted to a little chemical assistance both orally and anally. Plus, he was chucking the vodka down his throat like a new Prohibition was about to be declared. Izzy tried to confiscate the rather large tumbler full but Cal would always grab it back to take another gulp.

"I hope I'm doing the right thing," he said to Izzy and Derek.

"What, the drugs?" Derek asked.

"Them I'll need if I'm gonna let all these fuckers go through me. God, why couldn't I keep my big fat mouth shut?"

Izzy commiserated. "Your plan to make Buzz jealous just backfired, that's all."

"No, what I meant was, I hope fucking them gets it out of their system. I've had to fend them off all week. More than anything, I hope Buzz doesn't find out."

"I can't imagine the guys will tell. They're your dad's best mates," Derek said.

"Yeah, well god save me from mates like that," Cal replied.

"Besides," Derek added, "Some of them rely on your dad for their jobs or else rely on his patronage and contacts. They won't want to lose that. If it all falls apart, I'll tell your dad it was my fault and I talked you into it. I'll make up some bullshit about how I wanted you so badly but you wouldn't have me so I wanted to see you fucked into humiliation."

"That works for me," Derek said, adjusting his crotch.

Cal drew them into a group hug. "You guys are the best. You got extra candy if I need it during the night?"

Derek nodded.

"How many are expected?"

"We asked upwards of thirty…"

"Ouch," Cal smiled, clutching his ass.

"As expected, some of them weren't into group activity," Derek said.

"And others had more respect for your dad. Or else were scared of him," Izzy added. "Or scared of their boyfriends. Or wanted to bring their mates. But I'd say, with last-minute chickens, it'll be no more than fifteen tops."

"Still ouch. The most I've done is a baker's dozen before. I was sore for a week."

Holy fuck! I really didn't know my son at all. Maybe it was time to sit down and talk to him man to man.

"Does your dad know what a slut you are?"

"Were," Cal corrected. "For him I'll become a nun."

"Obviously not from an order where it's forbidden to open your mouth," Derek joked.

"Come on, let's do it. Get me lubricated, lads."

Cal dropped his shorts and bent over, pulling his cheeks apart, and his friends began lubing his asshole with a sticky grease, liberally smearing his insides as they pushed in their fingers to get at every little nook and cranny.

"It's water resistant, long lasting," Izzy said, reading from the label. "Also has a mild numbing effect."

"Hope it is only mild," Cal said. "If I'm gonna go through this, I want to at least feel it. The good bits, not the pain."

"What if they're all bottoms?" Derek joked.

Cal hit him playfully. "Not a problem for the first three, after that you guys might have to step in."

They laughed as they finished getting Cal's ass ready for the big event. The activity became more mundane after that and I took the opportunity to grab a beer and take myself in hand.

The guests were fidgeting, awaiting the arrival of the guest of honor. I heard the whistles and murmur of approval before I saw him, almost losing my load when he came into view. Cal was naked except for a thin sheen of oil all over his body, his cock covered by a scrap of fabric that left nothing to the imagination but which left his ass free. I marveled that the bloody thing stayed attached, especially as the crowd's obvious approval was exciting him. But the crowning glory of this magnificent spectacle was the slave collar wrapped around his throat, and the long chain by which Izzy led him to the pool area. Izzy and Derek were now clad in leather outfits like fascist military police. They were fuckin' hot and I noticed a few of the crowd give them the once over.

Izzy called for order.

"You all know why you're here so let's cut to the chase. Obviously, secrecy is paramount, so what goes on here tonight stays here. That's why we confiscated your mobile phones. No pictures."

I had a good laugh at that.

"That means no blackmail, no tattle tales, and Buzz never finds out."

There was a murmur of approval because there were a couple of heterosexually married men in the crowd.

"In a moment, Derek will hand you a card from the deck we've prepared. King high. Whoever gets the King card, goes first. The choice of what you do with or to Cal is up to you but the rules are strict. If he says 'no' you stop immediately. We'll have no hesitation in throwing out anyone who breaks the rules. There's to be nothing that leaves marks or causes injury, but if in doubt, ask. If you want to share then please feel free to invite the next cardholder to join you. All his orifices are yours to do with what you will. No fisting. And if Cal needs to take a break, then we'll ask you to leave him to rest for a while. Oh, the Ace is the wild card, and the man who gets it can choose whichever position on the running order that he wants. Got it?"

There was a mumble of general agreement.

As Derek attached Cal's slave collar and lead to a chain that ran around the pool area wall, Izzy handed out the cards. A few men groaned while others began stripping off their clothes.

"What if we want seconds?" a guy yelled from the crowd.

"Or thirds?"

Some of these guys intended staying for the duration.

"That's up to Cal," Derek said.

Cal smiled at his admirers, then slurred as he said. "Hell, why not? My body's yours until noon tomorrow. Do your worst."

There was a whoop of joy. Cal was pissed as a fart. Derek and Izzy looked at each other with concern. This could so easily get out of hand. Clothing removal became more frenzied until most of the men were naked, their different sized cocks drooling their approval.

"Anyone who arrives late," Izzy added, "Will go to the end of the queue. Enjoy yourselves, gentlemen."

A few of the men hurriedly took their blue tablets or some other chemical concoction while the lucky winner, a middle-aged guy who I recognized worked at my plant, milked his cock to get it hard. He whispered in Cal's ear and my boy went to the sun lounge and lay on his back with his legs over his head. There were whistles as he revealed his hot hole to the masses.

The plant worker was Greek, his body a mat of fur, his cock about average, his body fit but not overdeveloped.

"Yum," Cal said as he watched the man aim his cock at his hungry hole, and push.

I heard Cal's sharp intake of breath because the top pushed all the way in without pause. Not an auspicious start, but Cal adjusted quickly enough, wrapping his legs around the man's hairy back, attempting to draw him farther inside.

The opening gambit attracted a smattering of applause. Some men stayed to watch, others went inside for a refill, or to watch porn on the TV in the living room. There was no sense of urgency as it was only eight o'clock and it was obvious they were here for the long haul. There was a certain amount of bartering as men attempted to exchange their cards for one higher up or farther down the sex chain. I would have opted for the latter because I love to feel my cock slamming into a hole that's already been liberally hosed with spunk.

The initial group of men who worked over Cal were either very vanilla or else intimidated by the public atmosphere. They huffed and they puffed and they blew in one orifice or another, spurred on by Cal's drunken encouragement. He was feeling no pain. One of them 'skull fucked' his face and throat until his gag and drool hung in slimy rivulets from his chin. I was surprised that I didn't recognize some of these men and knew there was no way Cal could ever have insulted them when he was fourteen. Someone had put the word out. My suspicions, naturally enough, fell on Zach.

I estimated that the speed with which guys were lining up to take their turn that the party would be over in about an hour, but I reckoned without repeats. I should have noticed that the men who were married, had boyfriends, or were expected elsewhere made up the initial thrust of activity. A number of them left after planting their seed, some calling that they'd be back later.

The participants were getting hungry, needing something to soak up the booze they'd brought with them.

I was glad to see that Izzy had insisted it was BYOG otherwise my meager supply of alcohol would have run out hours ago and I didn't fancy paying for social lubrication so these men could fuck my boy.

Izzy and Derek served the pizza, the garlic bread, the soft drinks, and the chicken nuggets. The wafting smell of the food got my salivary glands pumping and I dug out the pizza I had brought in with me. I knew I'd be hankering for cheese and pepperoni. I love it cold which was just as well. So, while the guests hoed into the hot meal they'd paid for, Izzy and Derek had insisted on a fee for access, to pay for food, cleaning and other bits and pieces, I settled down to my cold repast.

Their entrepreneurial skills impressed me. I may have to offer them serious employment at my firm. What didn't impress me was that Luigi and his son, Tony, who ran my favorite pizzeria were somewhat gobsmacked by the scene they'd stumbled into upon delivering the vittels. They seemed in no hurry to leave, Luigi in particular running his hand over Cal's luscious rump, inserting a finger into his slimy hole.

Without so much as a by your leave, Luigi unzipped his trousers and fished out his long snake of a cock which looked obscene waving from his fly. He bent Cal forward, speared his ass, and knocked him onto the concrete pavers.

"Lift your ass, fag," Luigi spat. "That's it boy, squeeze your ass round my prick. You like thick Italian sausage, eh?"

If Tony was surprised by his father's behavior, he didn't show it. In fact, he also eagerly unzipped, lifted Cal's face to his cock, and rammed it home. Fuck, it was hot watching my boy spit roasted. I tugged at my own sausage as I watched, nibbling on the pizza I'd bought from Luigi the day before.

He was spitting out what I presumed were obscenities in Italian as he pounded Cal's butt, probably eager to get back to his shop, while Tony took a more leisurely pace, his motive becoming obvious when Luigi slammed into Cal and shuddered, his spunk obviously flooding my boy's guts. When he pulled out, demanding that Cal clean his slimy prick, pushing it into his mouth, Tony took over his father's anal position. He paced his fuck in order to make it last but, even so, it was over in less than five minutes. He wiped his prick on Cal's butt cheek before he zipped up.

As they left, Luigi yelled, "Save some of that ass for later, we'll be back."

Unless Izzy paid in advance or by credit card, Cal's ass was the price of catering. I did a quick calculation and realized Luigi had come out trumps, especially if, as threatened, he turned up for seconds. Hmm, I could probably use that to my advantage next time I wanted double pepperoni.

By this stage, Cal looked hungry for more than cock and went to help himself to a slice, his chain long enough that he could move freely around the yard but not escape it. Zach smacked his hand away.

"Uh huh," he said. "How about we give you a special topping, one that a slut like you would really appreciate?"

A couple of guys snickered as Zach aimed his cock at the large slice Cal had his eye on and began to wank. A couple of the others joined in and soon there was a regular pizza bukkake in progress.

"Oh, fuck yeah," Cal purred. "Cum pizza. Yum."

Cal's enthusiasm did knock the shine off Zach's attempted humiliation but, to give him credit, he kept at it, dumping a load of spunk atop the cheese. The other men followed quickly, the sperm puddling in the cheese crannies before oozing off the slice. Zach held it up for Cal's inspection. If he expected a shudder of distaste, he was disappointed as Cal placed his hand under the slice, lifted it high, catching the drools of cum hanging from the edges in his mouth and swallowing. When he'd cleaned up the edges, he took an enormous bite, chewing the gluggy mix with the sounds of unsubtle delight.

Finishing the slice in record time, he turned to his audience and fingered his ass. "Come on, guys," he begged. "I thought you wanted to fuck me into submission. Hell, I can take a lot more than you're handing out."

"Shut the fuck up, slut!" Zach snapped. Evidently, there was no love lost between these two.

"Why don't you use that thing between your legs and make me," Cal challenged.

That was like a red rag to a bull. Zach grabbed Cal roughly by the hair, forcing him to his knees, and then tried the rough 'hate fuck' routine except this time there was real hate involved. The bile and spite behind Zach's brutality were palpable. He'd dragged Cal closer to the shed, away from the crowd, so he could whisper.

"Listen you fuckin' piece of worthless slut trash. Leave Artie alone," Zach spat. "You hear me? Or next time I really will choke the fuck out of you."

Zach embedded himself in Cal's throat so he couldn't breathe, until he turned purple in the face. I could see his throat muscles working feverishly until Zach's eyes widened in surprise and he gasped as Cal siphoned his spunk into his belly. Zach attempted to pull away, muttering "No, no, not yet" but Cal held him tight until he'd milked him dry. Zach staggered back as Cal took a giant gulp of air, his face splotched with puke, cum and mucous. He glared triumphantly at Zach.

That's my boy!

Izzy came over to ensure he was all right, wiping his face and his watering eyes.

"You want I should throw him out?" Izzy asked.

"Nah," Cal coughed. "He's hated me ever since he found out Artie fucked me behind his back. Let him have his moment of triumph. I beat him at his own game." So saying he ran his tongue across his lips.

"You up for more?"

"Bring it on."

Zach's behavior worked as a bit of a dampener on the next few men who were far more solicitous of Cal than I expected. They asked after his comfort as they claimed his mouth and his ass until he stopped their concern by whispering, "I like it rough, daddy."

I was amazed by how many men believed those words were the green light to wrap their hands around his throat as they violently fucked him, calling him slut, whore, cunt and countless other humiliating names although that merely seemed to increase Cal's thirst for sex.

I'd already come twice watching his degradation, wondering at my own motives. I didn't hate my son; in fact, he was everything I looked for in an ideal mate. The fact that he seemed to be a total slut was even more in his favor. I'm not a man who takes to monogamy easily. It rhymes with monotony for a reason. I want a slut who takes orders, not someone who gives himself willingly to others behind my back. I didn't care that Cal had taken on Zach, whom I detested, or any other number of men I'd asked not to fuck him. What I cared about was that I hadn't been told.

From my hidey hole, I realized that what I wanted was to be out front, giving my tacit approval to his behavior, ordering him to obey my commands no matter how depraved. I guess I wanted to be Zach, without the nasty.

It was too late now to make an appearance. Besides, I still had to struggle with my conscience. Fuck the law, I had no time for that, but social niceties were much more deeply ingrained and would take a little getting over. I made a mental note to try hypnotism.

Artie was up next and the attraction between the two of them was obvious. Zach stood to the side watching closely.

"Hey, buddy. You mind if I fuck that beautiful hot tush of yours?"

Artie was the first to ask.

"For you, Artie, my ass is always available."

"Look, I'm sorry about Zach. He was too rough on you. I'll talk to him later."

"No, Artie. That will just make it worse. Let it lie. Just concentrate on fucking me like you did last time."

"God, you're such a hot piece of ass, Cal. I could fuck you all night."

"I wish you would, but I can see a boyfriend who'd have your guts for garters if you tried."

"Your dad didn't want us to fuck you, did he?"

I hoped Cal would keep his mouth shut. So far the only people who knew I'd fucked my own son were Izzy and Derek. Clive knew about the incident at the airport, believing it was the accident it was, not realizing it had continued. The last thing I needed was for the world to know what had been going on.

"I guess no dad wants to hear about his son or daughter being fucked by his best mates."

"When you put it that way."

"Zach is getting toey, better start with the curses, Artie. Maybe we can hook up next week or something."

"Cool," Artie purred, upping his volume to shout, "Take my cock right in your slut hole, boy. Feel my meat inside your guts. Gonna spew my spooge, breed you, slut boy."

Watching a muscle god like Artie pound Cal's ass was so hot, I blew a load just watching, merely holding my cock in my hand. This coupling would be a scene I'd watch repeatedly on my computer. God, I was so glad I took the trouble to set up my little porno studio.

What a lackluster lot my friends were on the whole. It was just in and out/in and out, blow a load, pat Cal's ass in appreciation and wander away for more grog. I understood why Phil's sleaze, Zach's anger, or Artie's soft loving might appeal. Occasionally, one of the other guys would pull hair, pinch nipples, bite a little too hard, curse such profanities that everyone would look up, but generally, it was all a bit tame.

Cal looked bored, egging them on to greater effort but they seemed to lose interest once they'd blown a load. Sure, a few came back for seconds, one of two of them for thirds, but it wasn't until an evil-grinning Zach returned while the others were inside watching porn, that the night really picked up.

"Aw, look who's all alone out here, no one to protect him. No big bad daddy. You're such a filthy whore. I bet Buzz doesn't know what trash you are."

"Are you man enough to tell him, Zach? I don't think so."

"Don't be so sure."

"Buzz would breed your ass so fast it'd make your balls curl."

"You really are just sub-human trash, Cal."

"That's why you want to fuck me, use me, and humiliate me."

Zach drove three fingers into Cal's sloppy ass, sawing in and out a few times before feeding him his slime-covered fingers. Cal sucked and licked them clean.

"Oh, I fully intend to do that, Cal. Your father will toss your ass out on the street so fast it'll make your head spin so you'll need a chiropractor just to suck cock."

"Why don't you feed me yours, Zach? Let me worship your big hard man prick. I know you love watching your cock slide into some young twink's mouth. Look good from up there, eh, Zach? Watching your dick slide over my tongue."

Zach did just as was hypnotically suggested, sliding his semi-hard monster into the waiting mouth, standing still for a few moments until Cal began to choke, piss dribbling down his chin.

"Drink it all, Cal, swallow it." Zach held Cal's nose as more piss squirted from his cock. He sprayed all over Cal's face and in his hair before aiming at his mouth again. "You stink, Cal. Stink of piss and stale spunk. You'll never wash that stench away. Buzz will smell it as soon as he gets back. Then your ass is toast."

Cal was shiny with piss and oil as Zach flipped him on his back, plunging his cock deep in his gaping asshole. As he pumped Cal's sluthole, other guests wandered out to the pool area for a closer look.

"Don't just stand there, you fuckers," Cal yelled. "Get your cocks hard. Spray your cum all over my face and body."

The guys were quick to obey, kneeling around various parts of his anatomy to dump their loads on his young, shiny skin.

"Drown me in your hot spooge. Scum all over my pretty slut face. Come on you two," Cal yelled at Izzy and Derek who were holding back. "Give me a load. I want to drown in spunk."

His two best mates joined the circle jerk, aiming their cocks at his tits as Zach rode his ass. The first blast of spunk hit his forehead making a track in his hair. One by one, they dumped a load until his face was a mess of so much spooge jelly he had to close his eyes to protect them. Zach wouldn't allow him to wipe the spunk away so he lay like a bukkake slut as his nemesis blew a load inside him.

"Okay, guys," Izzy said, zipping up his leather outfit. "Curfew for the next three hours until he recuperates." Leaning over his friend, he whispered, "Cal, you okay?"

"Never better, mate."

"Here's a towel to wipe your face. Call if you need anything."

"Thanks, Izzy. I'll be fine. I might take a dip in the pool."

"The chain's long enough for this end but you won't be able to go far," Izzy said. "But enough to clean up, though the amount of spunk on you, you'll probably clog the filter."

"You having fun?" Derek asked.

"Not as much as I thought. They're pretty boring. No imagination."

"Yeah, I noticed."

"You know who I wish was here?"

"Your dad."

"Yeah."

Izzy slapped his butt. "Get a rest. There's a few more turning up in the morning."

"Slip them something to kill their inhibitions."

"I'll see what I can do."

Cal lay quietly for a few moments covered in spunk. I heard Izzy lock the back door so my boy had some quiet time. Now was my chance. My cock was so sore from watching, it now needed some quality time. I retrieved an old rag from the back of the shed before slipping out onto the paved pool area.

My movements startled Cal and he reached for the towel to wipe his eyes.

"Leave it!" I said in my most commanding voice, hoping he didn't recognize me.

He obeyed.

Leaning over him, I licked the spunk from his eyes, swallowing it greedily. "Keep your eyes closed."

Wrapping the rag around his face, tying it tightly at the back of this head, I waved my hand but there was no reaction.

"Right, leave the blindfold on and we can have a bit of fun."

"Who are you?" he asked.

"Just someone who saw you in action through the back fence and wants a piece of that cute ass of yours."

"Help yourself," Cal invited.

"Oh, I intend to boy. An ass as good as yours should be shared around."

"You a friend of the guy who lives here?"

"Yeah, I know him well."

"I'm his son. Fuck me good and you can come visit any time."

I turned him over and buried my face in his spoogey asshole, excited at eating the loads of all my mates, especially the nasty dump from Zach. God, Cal's asshole was so ripe. I snuggled my mouth into his battered hole and sucked, punching my tongue inside. This was my boy, the one created from my spunk. I wanted to breed his ass, that fine boy ass.

Swallowing the slime, feeling it trickle down my throat, I kneeled, aiming my cock at his drooling asshole. I pushed, slid in, my cock surrounded by warm spunk. I tweaked his nipples, caressed his muscular arms, running my hands over his taut stomach muscles before gripping his cock. I'd seen him come twice while he was being fucked, most recently with Zach, but he was still hard. I don't think he'd been satisfied.

As I drove my prick ever harder into his squelching ass, I could feel his balls tighten in my hand. I was going to make my little boy come.

"Fuck me, daddy. Breed my slut ass," he panted. "Show me how a real man does it. Oh god, fuck me like an animal."

I scratched and bit and squeezed his body until I thought it would be black and blue, as battered as his red swollen ass cunt. My boy was born to be fucked. As I felt his ass muscles constrict around my cock, he shot his load into my fist. I moaned, in part from the incredible feeling in my balls as I unloaded inside my own son, but mainly because I knew I was addicted to him. I couldn't live without him impaled on my cock. And I didn't know of any clinic I could turn to for help with that addiction.

I was in heaven. And I was headed for hell.

SONNY SIDE UP

*I*n the end I was a coward. After I'd impaled a blindfolded Cal on my incestuous prick, spewed my spunk into his bowels, and made my boy spill his spooge all over my hand, I sneaked off without revealing my identity. By the time he removed the rag wound tight across his eyes, I was back in my cabin hideout watching him through one of the peepholes I'd drilled.

The remainder of the night and early morning was a real anti-climax. Well, truth be told there were enough climaxes as guys turned up for seconds and a few stragglers turned up for their first go at Cal. He slept most of the time, waking only for the half-hearted fuck that one of my erstwhile friends threw into him with all the finesse of a water buffalo tap dancing. Cal was bored, I was bored with him. And for him.

I slept too, drifting into oblivion while still organizing in my mind how I was going to escape my hiding place to reappear as the doting father returned from his business trip with no idea of what had occurred in my absence. It would be difficult to face some of my friends and employees after what I'd seen. It was none of my business really if they wanted to fuck my son, it was the underhanded and hypocritical way they'd gone about it. At the time it escaped me that was the pot calling the kettle…

Around eight o'clock in the morning Izzy and Derek lumbered into the back pool area, still hung over or else very tired from their chaperone duties. Cal, too, was groggy and obviously in some discomfort. He complained of his ass being sore so Derek rubbed cream into his butt hole which seemed to soothe him.

"That should numb the pain for a while at least," Derek said as they unlocked his chains.

"I made breakfast," Izzy said. "You probably should get some food into you and then try to get some sleep."

"Was that everyone?" Cal enquired.

Derek and Izzy swapped glances.

"Please tell me there are no more," Cal begged.

Derek reminded him, "The cut-off time was noon."

"And in a moment during which your desire was too big for your asshole, you invited people back for extra helpings this morning."

Cal groaned. "Send them away. Tell them I was fucked to death or something."

"You wish," Derek said. I thought I detected a whiff of disapproval in his voice.

Izzy might have, too, as he was quick to change the subject. "So, any of them keeping material?"

"Most of them were in real danger of boring me to death. And I use the word boring in the sense of dull and uninteresting, not as in drilling. There was Artie, of course, always reliable except for Zach, that disgusting boyfriend of his. Oh, and the stranger. Now, he was hot!"

Izzy sounded concerned. "Stranger?"

"Middle of the night. Everyone was asleep inside. He snuck up on me. Blindfolded me and pounded me just the way I like it. Wouldn't tell me who he was."

"He must have been someone at the party," Derek said.

"No. He said he'd watched through the back fence and got so turned on he had to have me."

They all turned to look at the fence.

"Plausible," Izzy said. "I guess he could have climbed over."

"Reckons he knows Buzz."

Derek sounded worried. "I hope he can keep his mouth shut."

Cal laughed. "Some of the things he did, I don't think he'd be spreading it around the neighborhood. He said he'd keep in touch. I hope so."

Izzy led the way inside. "Come and have breakfast before it gets cold."

Derek patted Cal on the butt. "And give your future a chance to heal."

As they went in via the glass doors, the front door bell echoed through the house. I quickly clicked the computer over to the living room spy camera, the furniture still covered in plastic sheeting in case the sexual activity had moved indoors. The visitor was Clive, my best mate. Why was he here? He knew I was out of town. The sound was fuzzy, but I thought I picked up the words 'my turn' and the rather insistent 'it's well before noon.'

I watched as Clive pushed his way inside. Derek pleaded with him. "Cal's really sore. It wouldn't be fair on him and it wouldn't be much fun for you."

"I don't give a shit about being fair," Clive snarled. This was a side of him I'd never seen before. "Was he fair when he threatened us all?"

"For Christ's sake, Clive, he was only fourteen." Izzy had come in from the kitchen.

"Anyway, he promised we could all have a go at his ass and," Clive tapped his watch, "I'm here well within the time." He held his hand up. "And before you tell me again that he's sore. Well, that just makes it all the better. I'm doing this as punishment, not pleasure. The little faggot's discomfort will make it all the better for me."

"I think you should leave," Derek said, standing up to him. Izzy was immediately at his side. It was a brave action but Clive could have them both for breakfast without breaking into a sweat.

The doorbell rang again. Clive smiled. "Ah, reinforcements."

Before they could stop him, Clive strode to the door, opening it to admit Zach and Phil, the two people I least wanted to ever see in my house again.

"Come in, guys. These two have just been telling me that our little faggot is sore this morning. Must have been some night. And that we should go easy, leave him alone. Maybe settle for a wank or a quick blow job because his lips are swollen. Both sets of lips, it seems."

The three of them cackled.

Clive took charge, turning to the new arrivals, "Take care of these two while I get the slut ready." He strode off toward the kitchen while Zach and Phil manhandled Izzy and Derek toward the stairs. I heard them struggle and scream as they were bundled upstairs, obviously to be locked in one of the bedrooms.

Clive dragged Cal into the living room by his balls, pushing him onto the floor, prodding him with his boot. "Turn over, slut. I want to watch your face while I fuck you."

"Come on, man. I'm fuckin' sore. I'll give you a rain check. Promise. It will be more fun when I'm not gritting my teeth."

"Not for me it won't." Clive was already stripping off his jeans, his boots and his top, getting ready for action. He was an impressive looking sight naked and Cal's eyes lit up. He ceased complaining, lying on his back, hoisting his legs in the air to give Clive access.

"You must be naturally lubricated by now," Clive smirked, shoving his fingers into Cal's butt hole, obviously trying to collect some of the spooge dumped in his guts during the long night of fucking. He smeared it along his cock shaft, Cal grimacing from the intrusion, his sphincter red raw.

Clive aimed his cock in the general direction of Cal's ass, then lunged to cause the maximum amount of pain. Cal yelped as the cock slid around the entrance to his swollen boy pussy before sinking into the warm depths of his anal tunnel. Clive didn't slow down for a moment, slamming his cock painfully in and out of Cal's battered body, as my son took deep breaths that signaled intense pain.

"You love cock so much, you'll worship mine by the time I've finished with you," Clive spat. "Last night was nothing, when we're done with you, you won't dare show your face around this town ever again. And your asshole will be mincemeat, not even fit for a fist. Me and my mates will make sure of that. So your dad fucked you the once and loved it, well mate, we're gonna fuck it whenever we want and there's nothing you can do about it. You don't dare tell daddy what you got up to last night because he'll throw you out on your ear. And once you move into the university, we'll phone you, tell you where to stand to be picked up by every sleazy fucker in town who wants a piece of cute boy ass."

"In your dreams, Clive. I'm only letting you fuck me because I promised but, come noon, you and your mates can go to hell for all I care. Yeah, you're right about one thing. I won't go squealing to dad. I brought this on myself and I'll take my punishment like a good slut. That's as far as it goes."

"Take my word for it, you'll be begging for our cocks before we're finished."

Just then Zach and Phil came back into the room looking smug.

"One of you guys put your cock in his mouth to shut him up, I'm sick of listening to the little cunt."

Phil was faster and soon had his cock buried down Cal's throat, choking him. Zach watched the frenzied activity stroking his cock, impatient to take his turn.

The vision on the computer went fuzzy, and then went black. I whacked it, prodding the keys in the hope of bringing the picture back to life, checked the connections, everything in fact I could think of, but the picture was gone.

Shit!

Cal could take care of himself and seemed unconcerned by Clive's threats but the situation could turn nasty real quick and I wanted to be able to intervene if necessary. I crept out of my hiding place to make my way quietly to the wall of the house, expecting at any moment that one of them might wander into the kitchen from which room I was in full view. I dared not enter the house in an attempt to free Izzy and Derek as I would be seen from the living room as I went upstairs, not agile enough to shimmy up the drain pipes, not that I knew which room they were confined in anyway.

My best bet was to monitor the action and prepare to step in at a moment's notice. Creeping along the wall I made it to the living room window which was open at the bottom, the gauze curtain giving me a perfect view inside the room while hiding me in the darkness of the surrounding bushes which was just as well as I realized I was totally naked.

The bombardment of filthy language continued, Cal now on his hands and knees sucking Zach's prick as he sat on the lounge, while Phil fucked his ass like a madman. Clive was shooting the action on his cell phone. He had to have blackmail in mind. Zach slam fucked Cal's mouth, holding the back of his head, his cock rigid in my son's throat as Cal began to turn red then purple in the face. When Zach finally released him, Cal coughed up phlegm and snot, his eyes watering. Zach grabbed him by the throat. "Next time you go anywhere near my Artie, I'll fuckin' choke you for real. Choke you till you run out of breath and I pump my spunk down your dead throat. Understand?"

Cal nodded. I suspect he would have agreed to anything at that stage.

"Peeping at something interesting?" a voice whispered in my ear, startling me.

Two cops hemmed me in, the older a big brute of a bastard in his fifties, the younger in his thirties hadn't gone to fat yet but was headed that way. They were both ugly shits with attitude to match.

"See for yourself," I suggested, wondering how the hell I was going to get out of this situation.

The older guy gawked at the action in the living room. "Holy shit!"

The younger guy kept an eye on me in case I bolted. "What's going on?"

"Three guys working over this young faggot. He's taking everything they dish out."

The younger man took a look and I saw my opportunity to scram. I got about three paces before the older of the two put his beefy arm around my neck. "Going somewhere?"

The men in the living room were making such a ruckus that they didn't hear us outside. I wasn't sure if this was a blessing or not.

The cops dragged me back to the window, both seeming eager to watch as much as I was, albeit for different reasons. Maybe not so different. My cock, hard from witnessing Cal's humiliation, poked against the young cop's thigh. He smacked it away. "Dirty bastard." However, I could see it was having the same effect on my two captors.

Phil's foul mouth was working overtime. "You love cock, huh? In your boy cunt, down your throat? You'll take all the cock we give you. You'll give us your sweet ass anytime we want. Won't you, fucker?"

Cal nodded as if in a trance. The cock in his ass was having the desired effect.

"Get up, fucker," Clive commanded. "Sit on Zach's cock. No, face him. Let him see the pain in your sweet eyes."

Cal held Zach's cock upright, impaling himself on it, shuddering as he sank to the balls.

"Now, Phil," Clive continued, "See if his ass ring will stretch to take your cock at the same time. If we're gonna work him over we might as well make it hurt."

"No, not that," Cal begged. "I'm in agony. I'll do anything, just don't do that."

"What are they gonna do to him?" the older cop asked.

"Double penetrate his ass," I whispered.

"You're kiddin' me?" the younger cop said.

"Watch."

Phil was pushing his cock against Zach's shaft, easing his prick into the tight sphincter that was doing all in its power to keep him out. It was a no brainer who would emerge triumphant. The roar of pain proved that Phil's brute force overcame Cal's reluctance.

"Fuck a duck," the older cop whispered admiringly. "He's got both cocks in his butt. That kid's got real talent in his ass."

"Maybe you'd like to try it for yourself?" I suggested. "Maybe both of you together."

I'd do anything not to be arrested, including pimping out Cal's sore ass.

The older cop seemed to hesitate before guffawing at the idea. "We ain't no faggots."

"Just because you stick your dick in a hot piece of available boy ass doesn't mean you're a faggot. You're only a fag if you take cock up your own butt." Oh, brother, was I laying it on thick. These idiots were just as likely to fall for that line of reasoning. Hell, anyone would to get his cock into Cal's beautiful butthole.

The young cop was more cautious. "Why would he let us tag him?"

"Listen to him."

Cal was turned on now that the two cocks were more comfortably wedged, stretching his ass lips to breaking point. "That hurts so good! Fuck me. Fuck me hard. Bust me wide open. Hurt me with those giant cocks of yours. Fill my butt with your hot slimy spunk."

Just then, Clive shut him up by sliding his dick between Cal's puffy lips, gagging him in both senses of the word. Cal was now just holes made to take cock, to swallow spunk, to fuck into submission.

The younger cop's voice was hoarse. "You still didn't answer my question. Why would he let us fuck him?"

I could see I'd have to lay it on even thicker. "You're both hot guys, he's a cock slut, you seem to have bigger than average in your trousers, he'd drool over you two."

The young cop was suspicious. "How do you know?"

"He's my…uh…flatmate."

The older cop was startled. "You live here?"

"Yeah."

The younger cop would take a lot more convincing. "So what are you doing out here then? Naked?"

"I took an early morning swim in the pool and got locked out. I heard Cal, that's the young guy's name, welcome visitors and, well, you've seen him in action, it's better than a porn movie. He doesn't mind if you watch, but some of his mates do."

"Like those three inside?"

"You got it."

"You ever fucked him?" the older cop asked.

"Ah…no," I lied.

The young cop was curious. "Why not?"

I took a deep breath. "He's my son."

Both men looked at me with a combination of awe and horror.

The young cop was open mouthed. "You get hard watching guys fuck your son?"

I had to be careful here. I had a very small bathroom window of opportunity. They could drag me down to the station and charge me as a Peeping Tom which means I'd go on the sexual offenders register, or, I could encourage them to fuck Cal thus blowing my cover but at least they'd let me go. Either way I'd be humiliated, although one would also leave me with a record. Another no brainer. As long as they never found out I'd fucked my own son. That would be really hot water. Steam-the-blackheads-right-out-of-your-nose hot. I took a chance.

"Yeah, but look at that. How could you not get hard. I don't look at him as my own flesh and blood but as a hole that needs to be filled with cock."

The young cop considered what I said. "Man, you are one sick dude." Then he smiled. "Tell you what. If that kid IDs you as his dad, then we may go easy on you. My wife doesn't do anal and, well, I always wanted to try. Never fancied boy butt before but, hell, that's one juicy ass. Right, Vinnie?"

Vinnie was having a hard time keeping up with the conversation as well watching the action. He nodded.

"What's your name?"

"Buzz."

"Well, Buzz. How do we know you aren't setting us up? Some people would do anything to cast us cops in a bad light."

"I guess they would, uh…"

"Roy."

I didn't dare offer money, so I lobbed the ball back in their court. "What did you have in mind?"

His face twisted into a sort of malevolent sneer. "Something so sick and twisted it would probably appeal to someone like you."

I knew exactly where this was going. I suspect Roy was also describing himself when he used the words 'sick and twisted.' Who am I to judge?

Our further negotiation was interrupted by a cry from the living room. We all turned our attention back to the action. Clive pulled his prick from Cal's mouth and spewed wads of spunk all over his face and in his hair. He wiped his cock on Cal's lips, forcing him to lick it clean. A few minutes later, Phil was panting his approaching orgasm, stabbing his dick into Cal's ass, the friction along Zach's shaft enough to bring them both off almost simultaneously. They were anything but quiet as they shot into Cal's buggered guts.

Phil pulled out and then Cal lifted himself gingerly off Zach's prick, his asshole gaping, spooge running down the back of his legs. They both offered their pricks to Cal to suck clean before they began dressing.

"Sorry to fuck and run," Phil crowed triumphantly. "But got a wife at home about to drop a bundle any day. You know how it is."

Clive tried to act superior. "How you gonna explain the cum all over your face and leaking out your ass to Buzz when he sees you?"

Cal just shrugged his shoulders.

Zach answered for them all. "You know what? We don't give a monkey's. Besides, he better get used to seeing you like this."

Roy had given me a sideways glance when Clive had mentioned my name. Obviously it corroborated part of my story.

"Come on, let's get the hell outa here," Clive said. "Before Buzz gets back."

"Till next time," Phil called back as they slammed the door.

Cal slumped on the lounge. To our surprise, he began to play with his cock. He was still horny. He hadn't got off.

"Come on guys, before he loses interest," I said shoving Roy toward the kitchen door, giving him a quick plan of action. I rapped loudly before ducking into the cabin to retrieve my shorts and T-shirt. "He likes it rough. Okay?"

Roy and Vinnie mumbled assent.

Cal must have believed it was Izzy and Derek knocking because he hadn't bothered to dress or clean himself up to any great extent when he came out to see what the noise was. I stood behind the peep hole in the cabin watching. Cal opened the door cautiously.

"Yeah?" he said.

"You're a bit of a mess, son," Roy said in a fatherly fashion. "Everything all right? Neighbors complained about a bit of a ruckus coming from this property. Mind if we come in and have a look?"

"Um, I'm not really dressed for company," Cal said.

"In fact, you're not dressed at all," Vinnie added.

Cal was tense. "Is that a problem? I am in my own home."

Roy was reassuring. "Not at all. What you get up to in private remains just that. Private."

Cal opened the door, standing aside as they entered. I waited until I saw them go into the living room then crept out of my hiding place. Roy had ensured the kitchen door was left unlocked. I heard voices in the lounge room.

"It's a mere formality, son," Roy said as I peeked around the door. "Just bend over, this won't hurt a bit."

"Aren't you going to wear gloves?"

"I'm allergic to rubber," Roy replied, kicking Cal's legs apart. "Spread your cheeks."

Cal sighed, leaning over the lounge. Roy sank two fingers into Cal's leaking hole. "Very wet, son. There's more cream in there than you'd find in a dairy." He retrieved his fingers, sniffing them. "Smells like man spooge. What do you think, Vinnie?"

To my surprise, Vinnie licked Roy's fingers. "Definitely spunk, sir."

Cal stood up for his rights. "It's not against the law."

"No one said it was, son," he said as he slipped his fingers back into Cal's gaping cavern, sawing in and out attempting to find Cal's prostate, as he kept up the conversation. "It could be camouflage to turn us off looking any farther, but we are true professionals."

"True professionals, sir," Vinnie reiterated.

These two were so good they could get a job in Vegas in sleaze stand-up comedy.

I'm not sure what Cal thought was going on but he kneeled patiently while the two cops took turn about finger fucking his ass while the other stripped. Vinnie was a hairy bastard with a bit of a paunch but a fine thick cock which, under normal circumstances, Cal would enjoy in his butt. Roy was fitter, wiry and muscular but going to seed. Both were on the homely side, not someone you'd pick up in a bar for their looks. Rugged just about sums it up. But what they were doing with their fingers was sure doing it for Cal. He wriggled his butt in an effort to get them to plug him harder and deeper.

"You're a bit of a slut, son?" Roy asked slipping his cock straight into Cal's hole once Vinnie had removed his fingers. There was no preparation or warning, just a quick slide into that warm sloppy hole.

Cal grunted, his sphincter must have been rubbed raw but he was still aroused enough that he began to push back against the invading prick, urging Roy to fuck him harder.

"Feel good, does it, son?"

"Oh, yes, daddy. Feels so good in my slut ass. Fuck me good, daddy. Fuck me hard."

"There won't be any accusations of police brutality, will there, son?"

"No, daddy. Just hold me down and fuck me."

"Why don't you feed him your cock, Vinnie? Let him get a taste of real man meat."

Vinnie seemed to be the kind of guy that needed someone to tell him what to do, but once the command went out he hopped to it. He seated himself on the back of the lounge pulling Cal's face onto his cock. From my vantage point I took enough footage on my phone as security in case I needed it, but the way the two cops were mounting my son I had no doubt they'd be repeat business.

I could tell that although he was turned on, Cal was tired, his reactions on automatic as he attempted to show the guys a good time. Fortunately, they weren't about to last long and Roy squirted a load along with a string of expletives about the relative merits of Cal's ass and his wife's reluctance to share same before he pulled out, his cock sensitive as it popped free. Vinnie all but pushed him aside in his eagerness to take his turn, perhaps afraid that Cal was too sore to continue.

He was not as verbose in his appreciation as Roy but made almost as much noise merely grunting and exhaling loudly. I didn't want to interrupt before he'd come so I was hoping, for Cal's sake, Vinnie was a premature ejaculator. He wasn't, it took him twice as long as Roy to orgasm. No sooner did I hear Vinnie huffing and puffing, watching his body shudder to a halt, I banged the back door and called, "Anybody home?"

"Shit, that's my dad."

I entered the room as Cal panicked, searching everywhere for something to hide his nakedness, managing only to find a pillow which he held in front of his crotch, while Roy and Vinnie took their time putting on their clothes. Pretending to be astounded by the scene in front of me I demanded, "What the hell's going on here?"

Roy flashed his police badge. "Police, mate. We received a complaint from neighbors about strange noises from this house and we came to investigate. We were obliged to give this lad a thorough cavity search in case of drugs."

"You often use your cock for that sort of search?" I asked sarcastically.

"Only when the cavity is as smoking as this lad's. Take a look for yourself." Roy spun Cal around, pushing his face into the lounge and parting his cheeks.

"That's an awful lot of spunk for just the two of you," I said, winking at Roy as Cal could not see me.

"I'm afraid we may have interrupted some rather obscene behavior by the young lad with person or persons unknown."

"Cal?"

"It's okay, dad. I'll explain everything later."

"Your asshole is quite swollen. Are you okay?"

"Fine, dad."

"Are you this boy's father?" Roy almost sounded convincing in his interrogation.

"I am."

"We've seen a lot of sick and twisted things in our line of work, haven't we Vinnie?"

"Yeah, boss."

"But one thing we've never seen, is a father fuck his faggot son in the butt. I imagine it would be just about the most cock hardening experience ever. You get my drift."

"You perverts want to watch me fuck my own boy in the butt?"

"Uh huh."

I was faux indignant. "What sort of sick bastards, are you? Can't you see he's suffering?"

"If you won't co-operate, we can always find a stash of drugs hidden somewhere in your house and cart you both down to the station. Won't look good on your records."

"You won't find any hard drugs in the house," I said.

"Oh, yes, we will," Vinnie retorted. "We'll *lend* you some just to make it look authentic."

"I can't afford to have a drug arrest on my record, dad," Cal pleaded. "What have we gotta do, sir?"

"Vinnie and I just want to watch your dad plug that sweet ass of yours while we watch."

"Then you'll leave us alone?"

"Uh huh."

"Come on, dad. Let's get it over with."

I stuttered. "I...I don't think I can. Not my own son.

"Just try," Roy demanded.

I shucked my clothes to reveal my rigid prick which gave the lie to what I had been saying. Normally, I would have plunged right in but I knew Cal was hurting.

"Lie on your back, son," I instructed and Cal lay down, pulling his legs over his head.

Kneeling behind him, I pressed gently against his slimy hole and my cock slid in easily.

Cal was suddenly hard himself.

"That feels so good, dad."

"I can't believe I have my cock inside my own son." I kept up a running commentary on what perverse pleasure I was getting from fucking my own boy and how gratifying his hole was. The cops seemed to buy it.

I noticed Roy take shots of our activity on his mobile phone as Cal wrapped his legs around me, urging me on. The candid photographs were enough to keep us both in line if we had any intention of following up with a complaint. We didn't. I was happy just to extricate myself from a situation that had been fraught with ignominy and humiliation, if not jail time.

"This is hot, boss," Vinnie said, adjusting his crotch.

"I wish we could stay. There's nothing more enduring than the love between a father and his son, especially when he's fucking that son up the ass. We have all we need," Roy said, tapping his phone for emphasis. "Security." I nodded my understanding. He extracted a card from his wallet and placed it on the coffee table.

"Son, if any bastard ever gives you any trouble, give me a call. We'll sort him out for you."

Cal seemed actually touched by the offer. "I appreciate it. Expect to hear from me. Even if it's just to show my thanks to both of you, show you a much more exciting time when my rear is not so battered."

"We look forward to it," Roy said, and the two cops disappeared out the front door.

"Dad…"

"I know." I pulled out.

"It's not that I don't want you to fuck me. I want it more than anything."

"After those two guys, you're just a bit sore. Right?"

"Uh…yeah."

"But you're still horny," I said, caressing his erection. I slid to the floor to take care of him because no one else had bothered. Wrapping my lips around his smooth young prick, I licked and sucked, tickling his balls, rubbing my thumb around his sphincter without penetrating, until he blew his wad in my mouth, forcing me to swallow his warm nut juice.

I carried him upstairs and lay him on the bed to rest while I ran a bath, adding liberal amounts of relaxing perfumed bath salts to soak the fatigue and aches from his body. As the tub filled, I released Derek and Izzy, explaining briefly what had happened with the police. They were ropeable about Clive, Zach and Phil's behavior, ready to exercise vigilante justice. I calmed them down and got them to pamper Cal, bathing him, toweling him down and putting him to bed.

Then I lay down in the quiet of my own bedroom listening to the three mates whispering their secrets down the hall. I was exhausted so I could imagine how Cal felt.

I couldn't keep up. Much as I loved Cal as a son, and as a sexual partner, I was glad he was heading off to university to be his own man, to live his own life. That was as it should be.

Sure, I would miss him. I just didn't realize how damn much.

ECLIPSE OF THE SON

Cal bounced back from his ordeal within a day of it being over, although I suspect his ass was still tender and he had a tendency to keep clearing his throat for the first few hours after he bounded down the stairs, bright as a spark, to ask, "You know of any dudes around your age who live around here who might possibly be gay? Maybe married, I'm not sure."

"You trading me in?" I asked.

"What's to trade, old man? You won't succumb to my ample charms, so I will have to look elsewhere."

He made himself some toast and coffee, that's all he seemed to eat at this hour unless someone else made breakfast for him.

"You know why we can't keep doing it, Cal. Much as I would love to. If your mother ever found out…"

"But she won't, will she?"

"All you need is someone like that bastard Zach to find out, and he'd be on the phone to her so fast your asshole would be turned inside out. It's me that would be in trouble, not you. I'd end up with a record, and a reputation as a sex offender, have to register wherever I went. And they wouldn't let me anywhere near you."

"Let's run away to Europe. No one knows us there."

"Stop dreaming, Cal. Come down out of the clouds and visit the real world."

"Stop lecturing me. You sound like mum."

"Maybe that's because I'm your dad. Dads are supposed to lecture and annoy their sons – not fuck them!"

He must have decided to change the subject before I became even angrier. "So, what about any gay neighbors?"

"None that I know of, but I'm not always the most reliable at sussing out fellow homosexuals." I was trying to be funny. It didn't succeed.

"Shit!" he cursed.

"Come on, out with it. What's going on?"

He hesitated, obviously gathering his thoughts. I was interested to see what he would come up with. It was good. If it had been an essay, I would have given it an A+.

"On the weekend while you were away…"

"Yes," I said, acting suspicious. "You didn't have a loud party or something, did you?"

"No, nothing like that," he lied, although strictly speaking the party hadn't been all that loud. "But on the Saturday, I was tanning beside the pool, naked as usual; I must have got a bit excited and started playing with myself." He looked at me to gauge my reaction.

"That's natural for someone your age. I was always attacking my dick twenty years ago. Still wanking every chance I get."

"I wish you'd let me do it for you." He sounded irritated. "Anyway, when I finished I rolled over to tan my butt cheeks and my back and I must have fallen asleep in the heat because the next thing I know I feel this guy on top of me fingering my ass."

"That doesn't mean he's from around here, you know. Perverts sometimes travel for miles to find their prey."

"But he wasn't a pervert. He was good, very good. Wouldn't let me see who he was. Tied a cloth around my eyes then fucked the shit out of me. Said he'd been watching through the fence while I was…uh…while I jerked off. Said it excited him so much he had to have me so he clambered over the back fence and got stuck into me. He didn't rape me or anything. I was more than willing. He had a nice cock. At least it felt nice, I didn't actually see it, or his body, or him. He said he lived around here, and knew you."

"Unless you can narrow it down a bit more than all the men under what?"

"Let's say 50 to be on the safe side."

"Okay, fifty it is. Unless you can narrow it down a bit more than all the men under 50 and over 18 in the radius of so many square miles, I'm afraid I can't help."

"I've asked Derek to see if anyone he knows has Grindr then we can walk around and see if anyone pops up."

"Just be careful, that's all I ask." I knew full well he wouldn't find his phantom lover because it was me. But you never know what dangers lurk for the unsuspecting. Had the man he was seeking so badly not been me, I might have been jealous at this point.

"Good fuck, was he?" I asked.

"He reminded me of you a lot," he said, but he didn't betray any sign that he actually knew it really was me. I didn't get the impression he was testing me.

"I suppose I should be pleased. I think."

He had been standing at the counter munching his toast but now came over to perch himself in my lap. He put his arms around my neck. "Dad. Why can't I live at home and go to uni? It would save money, I could help you out around the home, you like my friends—"

"Derek and Izzy at any rate."

"You have a pool."

"Stop right there. You have never helped out around the house since you moved in. Yeah, damn right I've got a pool which you refuse to help clean. Besides that, you're disruptive, you cause me problems with my friends—"

"I was drunk. It won't happen again."

"I've heard rumors that in fact it did. That Zach guy has a vicious tongue. For the moment I accept that he is just trying to cause trouble…"

Cal blanched, resting his head on my shoulder so I couldn't see his guilt.

"Once classes start I won't have time to be disruptive. It'll be work, work, work. I'll stay home. It will save money on accommodation, entertainment and bar hopping because each night I'll be snug in bed with you."

"Nice try, buster," I said jiggling him off my knee so he almost fell on his ass on the floor. "Did you ever think I might need a little me time? With you around that's almost impossible."

He pinched my nipple so hard I grimaced. "If that's the way you feel, prepare yourself for me to fall to pieces. I mean it."

I didn't like the way this conversation was ending.

"Cal. Come here, mate."

He stood in front of me with that hang-dog look he's perfected when he doesn't get his own way. It's remarkably successful but it doesn't work on me. I backed him up against the kitchen bench, pressing against him. I put my arms around him. "You know I love you Cal."

"Just not the way I want you to."

"Yeah, I do. God help me, but I do."

"Then why—"

"I'll make you a deal. You do good work in your studies, get good grades, you and me will go away together during the long break, work something out together, maybe move you back home."

"A year? Are you fuckin' kidding me? I'll never last that long."

"You'll just have to try. And Cal, just maybe you'll find yourself a nice man who you'll fall in love with and he'll fall in love with you and he won't be one of my friends."

Much as he complained, Cal must have liked the idea because his spirits picked up immediately. "I've already got me one of those."

That was the first I'd heard of it. "Who?"

"You," he said smugly, squeezing the erection that was poking into his crotch.

He genuinely settled down over the next few days, actually helping around the house, but I could see the effort was nearly killing him.

Life moved on. I would eventually have to address what I had seen at the gangbang, but I needed to think it through calmly, no use flying off the handle. I needed to make it work to my advantage.

The minor players, like some of the guys from the factory floor, I'd let slide. Sure, they'd been opportunistic but I wasn't convinced I would have acted any differently in their situation. Closer to home, I had to worry about Artie. He was the first I called into my office.

"Come in, Artie."

"Something wrong?"

"You tell me?"

"What do you mean?" He could be so innocent sometimes.

"Zach is spreading rumors. About Cal."

"Aw, shit. I told him it would get me into trouble. I'm sorry, Buzz. I'll have a word to him."

I passed over a coffee and Danish, just the way he liked them. It helped him relax. I watched him as he ate and sipped his coffee. He watched me watching him and it wasn't long before he got nervous, his hands shook and he had to put the cup back on my desk or spill the contents.

"Ah, fuck, you know, don't you?" he whimpered in defeat.

"Know what, Artie?"

"You know me and Cal is seeing each other, don't you?"

"Does Zach?"

"No, he'd have Cal's balls for ear-rings if he did."

"You like Cal?"

"Look Buzz, I don't like lying and I don't like creeping around behind your back. Yeah, I like the little bastard a lot. But I don't love him. We just have this chemistry. It's just fun, that's all. Neither of us means anything by it. I said we should tell you but he thought you might fire me. So, go ahead. Who told you? It wasn't Cal?"

"No, it wasn't Cal. And, no, I'm not going to fire you. Thanks, Artie, that's all."

He looked so relieved to escape my office. I called him as he was about to go out the door.

"Oh, Artie."

He tensed, probably expecting a blow of some sort because it had all been too easy.

"I don't mind if you want to keep seeing Cal. It's up to him who he sees, but if you hurt him, I'll come down on you like a ton of bricks."

"I would never hurt Cal," he said earnestly, but I already knew that.

"One last thing. The company has been growing too big for me to handle everything on my own. I'll have to be a little more management and a little less hands-on in future. So I'll need a 2 IC, a sort of foreman of the foremen. You know what I mean?"

"Sure, Buzz." He thought about it for a moment. "You know who'd be really good. Blackie in the—"

"No, you don't understand, Artie. I'm offering the job to you. If you want it."

"Me? After you found out I'm fucking...um... seeing Cal?"

"You think you could handle it?"

He puffed his chest out. "Fuck, yeah. You watch me."

"Come and see me after work this afternoon and we'll go out for a drink, discuss your new wages and conditions."

That meeting, at one of the quieter gay bars, turned out quite propitiously. Artie and I were comfortably ensconced in one of the booths and we just sorted through his new duties and his new remuneration package when Zach stormed into the place. He saw us and made a beeline for our table, ensuring that he made enough of a commotion that everyone would be watching.

"There you are," he screamed at Artie. "I can't trust you out of my sight for a minute. What the fuck are you doing here? I was expecting you home an hour ago."

"I'm having a drink with Buzz to celebrate my new position with the company."

"About time is all I can say. I hope he's paying you good money, not those lousy pay slips you've been bringing home lately. Wouldn't keep a duck in feathers."

"Very good money, Zach. Probably more than I'm worth." He turned to me. "I'm gonna make sure you never regret giving me this opportunity."

"Stop brown nosing all your life. It's no more than you deserve and he knows it. If you'd taken my advice you would have left his shitty company years ago. You'd be a boss by now."

Artie thumped the table. Everyone in the bar looked over. "Why can't you be happy for me, Zach? Just once, be happy for me."

Because Zach didn't want Artie to be happy. You could see it written all over his face. What he said next confirmed it. "I suppose the whole thing is a bribe so you won't fuck his little boy anymore."

Artie looked at me and I nodded my approval. I marveled that he was so even tempered and calm. "As a matter of fact, Zach, he knows about me and Cal. And Buzz has given his okay for me to keep seeing him for as long as the two of us want."

Zach turned on me. "Ha! The joke's on you, Buzz. I made Artie promise to give up that little tramp whore son of yours."

Artie's arm shot out so quickly, grabbing Zach around the throat, that some bar patrons actually gasped. I looked over at Greg, the barman who pointed at the phone. It was a hotline to the cops. I smiled and shook my head. He smiled and went back to watching the action. It was better than what was showing on the TV above the bar.

Artie spoke through gritted teeth. "You will never, ever, speak like that about Cal again. When I let you go, you will apologize to Buzz for saying those things about his son. As for the promise, let's just say I consider it null and void because you promised me you wouldn't go spreading vicious rumors again. But I heard you on the phone just yesterday. When you stop spreading rubbish, I'll stop seeing Cal. Deal?"

Artie let go of Zach who gasped for breath and rubbed his neck as if he'd been choked.

"Don't milk it, Zach. You're a terrible actor. Apologize."

Someone at the bar laughed.

Zach turned to me, his eyes blazed hatred. "I regret if you were upset—"

Artie's hand pulled Zach face down onto the table. He snarled. "The only person who really will regret it, Zach, is you. I said apologize."

I got an apology in the end. I didn't require it, but it was good to see Artie standing up for himself. When it was all over, he shook my hand and thanked me for the opportunity I'd given him, then frog-marched Zach out of the bar, informing him there would be a serious discussion when they got home.

The bar gave a collective sigh of relief now that it was all over and the patrons got back to what was foremost on their minds: picking up a fuck. I must have been one of the very few who was not there for that reason although I had obviously attracted enough attention to have a guy sidle up to the booth and ask if he could buy me a drink.

As the adrenaline was still pumping, I accepted. It had been a while since I had been out like this. The guy was rugged but good looking, a few years younger than me and from the cut of his jib very respectably put together. Maybe I could score. I'd put that side of my life on hold since Cal moved in. With his departure imminent, there was no time like the present to get my skills sharpened.

Jack, my pick-up was very pleasant company and we left the bar together about two hours later to go dancing at a gay club nearby. By the time we rolled back to my place it was around midnight and the house was in darkness. Cal was either out or asleep. Either would do.

We headed straight for my bedroom and after a bit of a tussle over who would fuck who, we compromised: I would fuck him first and then he would have a go at my ass. We both agreed that would be a satisfactory outcome. He begged to use the bathroom and from the look on his face it would be embarrassment all round to use the en suite so I steered him to the one down the hall.

He sure took his time but I understood if he hadn't intending going bottom this evening then…eventually he was gone so long I went in search. Of course, I knew what I was going to find, it was inevitable.

The bedside lamp was on, I would have said deliberately, so it was easy to watch Cal in action. I had no intention of standing hidden in the shadows, cock in hand, watching my pick-up ram his prick up my son, so I stood squarely in the doorway. Jack had a way with words, certainly, and he had positioned Cal on his back with his legs splayed giving him the finest access to his ass. He was taking every advantage of that access, slamming his prick in with as much force as possible.

"Fuck, your ass is hot, kid. So fuckin' hot. It could singe the hair on my balls if I let it. You like it really rough, eh? Me, too. I could fuck you all night, maybe I will, empty my balls in you three or four times. The guy down the hall wanted to fuck me but I'm not really into that. Glad I saw you before I went back to his bedroom. Who is he, mate? Your boyfriend? Sugar daddy? Eh?"

"He's my dad," Cal said when he could catch the breath that was being knocked out of him at every plunge.

"Sugar daddy, eh?"

"No, my real dad."

"Fuck me. Your old man is gay as well? He knows you're gay, right? Shit, you know what would be really cool? To watch you two make out. Fuck, makes me wanna come just thinking about it. How could he resist this ass of yours? Made to be fucked and fucked hard and fucked often. Think we could interest your dad in a threesome? That would be so perverted."

Jack was working his jaw big time but he must also have been working his cock deep in Cal's ass because neither of them had noticed me standing watching. They were in a world of their own. And bugger me, if I didn't have a hard-on. No matter how much I tried to keep it down, it always reared its head whenever Cal was around. I was on the verge of joining in. Fuck the humiliation of losing my pick-up to my son.

"You know a guy named Phil? He was the one who said I should pick up your dad, showed me his photo, and said 'Pick up the dad. Go back to his place. Down the hall is the sweetest piece of boy ass ever! Once you fuck it you'll never want anyone else.' Phil's your biggest fan. Says one day he's gonna organize the biggest gangbang ever. Get you listed in the Guinness Book of Records. I'd love to see that."

On the mention of the name Phil, Cal's eyes opened wide and he saw me standing in the doorway. I couldn't make out the emotions that flickered across his face and he said nothing as Jack kept rambling while ramming his ass. Then Cal must have thought better of worrying about me because he closed his eyes again and surrendered to the cock inside him.

I closed the door and went back to bed, still awake and grinding my teeth about an hour later when I heard the front door close. A few minutes later I heard Cal in my doorway. I pretended to be asleep because I couldn't bear to speak to him tonight. He whispered, "Dad, you awake?" then repeated it. When I didn't respond he sighed and padded down the hallway to his own bedroom.

He was still asleep when I got up the next day and I made sure I was gone before he came down for breakfast. Later at work, I didn't answer his calls when my home ID came up on the landline and the mobile.

I brooded all morning which was not helping the company, but I could think of no way of getting Phil to back off without hurting his wife, Helen. That reminded me that I had to find a replacement – and fast! Helen had been gone almost a week but I'd done nothing about it. I searched the computer for agencies and came across one that seemed reputable, offered references and 24-hour turn-around. I explained my requirements to a charming woman who answered the phone and I heard her clacking away at her own keyboard. She hadn't sounded hopeful. "It's very short notice. It's a busy time of the year, you understand, but I'm sure we'll have someone on the books that will suit you. There's…no, retired I think. She's married, bringing up kids. What about…no, totally unsuitable." She was chatting to herself so I drew caricatures of Phil with arrows stuck through his head, knives in his chest, the sort of thing that would get me arrested for murder if he just happened to drop dead in the next week or so.

"Here we are," she said, oozing confidence again. "I just knew I'd find someone suitable. Jean Hudson. Comes highly recommended. Fairly new to the agency. Young, but highly qualified. I'll call about availability and ring you back."

She was as good as her word and informed me that Jean Hudson would be at my office nine o'clock sharp in the morning.

At least something went right that day.

When I got home I discovered just how wrong things could go that day as well. There was no sign of Cal. In fact, there was no sign he had ever lived there. His room was empty. There were no farewell messages; it was as if he never existed. I was tempted to ring his mobile but after the way I'd treated him today I doubted he would answer. I convinced myself that it was for the best. My life had been in turmoil since he arrived. Now I could look forward to some equilibrium.

Who was I kidding? The house was lonely and depressing without him. I found myself in bed earlier than usual, massaging my cock to the computer movie of his gangbang near the pool. I went to sleep believing it would have been better for everyone if Cal had never come back into my life.

That dark mood lasted until 9am on the dot the next morning when Jean Hudson turned up for work. Jean was oh so my type. Young, clean cut, collegiate, couldn't have been more than twenty-two or twenty-three, body squeezed into clothing so tight the stitches had to be of the strongest thread because the muscles threatened to burst them apart. Gorgeous beyond belief. And he spelt his name Gene.

He brought sanity back into my life. With Cal gone, the irregular hours, the partying, the jealousy, the squabbling with friends, all dried up although at the back of my mind I still had to take care of unfinished business with Zach, who had gone quiet since his hissy fit at the bar. I didn't trust him not to have some foul scheme hatching. Then there was Phil, my secretary's supposedly homophobic straight husband, and my erstwhile closest buddy, Clive, all of whom had piled on to Cal's steaming ass. Okay, he'd drunkenly invited it but you don't fuck your mate's son. No matter how much you want to.

Gene needed training. I'd hoped Helen would be up to the task but I'd left it too late, like I do sometimes, and she'd already gone on maternity leave. I'd have to do the training myself. It would be an unexpected pleasure. Gene was very easy on the eye, and my imagination informed me he'd be very easy on the cock as well. I had to shake the image out of my head. I couldn't bring myself to call him a secretary or a receptionist, so I settled for assistant. Each day I looked out at him working at his desk through the glass panel that separated our two offices.

Gene often looked up from his computer to catch me staring. He always acknowledged it with a smile. Zing! That smile went straight to my cock. I squeezed it under the desk, wondering whether I had time to draw the Venetian blinds and whack out a spray.

Working so closely together, especially in the early training period, I suppose it was inevitable that I invited him out. He was new to the city, comparatively friendless, although with his good looks and effervescent personality he wouldn't remain so for long.

I was toying with the idea when Artie turned up. He stopped long enough to shoot the breeze with Gene then ambled into my office.

"I know I shouldn't say this, Buzz, but that is one sweet receptionist you got yourself."

"I told you before; I thought he was a girl because of his name."

"No way would you mistake him for a girl if you got a good look at that package between his legs."

"You're a married man, should you be peeking?"

"No peeking involved. It's out there as blatant as daylight. He's got a hard-on and he's advertising. As for being married. Hmm, not so sure. Zach's got a bit stand-offish lately and, you know what?" He was about to say more but must have thought better of it. "Skip it, it's not your concern."

"It is if it will affect your work."

He shook his head. "Won't let it do that. This job is too important to me."

"That's what I wanted to talk to you about." I stood and signaled to Gene to bring in the papers I'd asked him to search out for me earlier. He knocked before he entered, then stood with his crotch, bulging obscenely in his tight trousers close to Artie's face as he lounged in the more comfortable chairs I had for visitors. I couldn't help but notice.

"Thanks, Gene," I said, attempting to unscramble my brain and get back to the business at hand.

"Anything I can do for either of you two gentlemen?" Gene asked, openly flirting.

"Uh...not at the moment. I'll let you know."

After Gene left, closing the door behind him, Artie smirked. "Now, tell me you didn't notice."

"It's hard to miss," I agreed. "Does he flirt with all the men like that?"

Artie thought about it. "I've seen him on the floor of the factory. You'd think the guys would give him shit and, yeah, one or two of them do, but I got onto that quick smart. The others quite like him. He knows everyone by name, pretty impressive because he's only been here, what?...a couple of weeks."

"Keep an eye on him for me, Artie. Let me know if there's anything...unusual."

"Will do."

We went over the business at hand, mainly about a section of the factory that was under-performing. It was the first big test I'd given Artie and I was keen to see how it played out.

I did finally pluck up the courage to invite Gene out. It became a regular Friday night ritual and we were seen together in all the right gay places. People began to talk. He was great company and he helped take my mind off Cal.

My son and I had parted on less-than-friendly terms but neither of us had contacted the other to make amends. As time went on, apart from the occasional twinge wondering what he was up to at the moment he didn't feature very largely in my thoughts. My wife was no longer ringing to check his progress so she must be in mobile contact with him and know he's no longer with me. I had to assume that if there was a problem she would ring, no doubt accusing me of being its cause. What saddened me more than anything was that Derek and Izzy didn't bother to keep in touch, not because of the tumbles in bed we'd once shared, but because I thought of them as friends.

I suppose it was inevitable that Gene and I would end up in bed together. I thought he was gorgeous and he thought I was hot. So we were meant for each other. We spent time talking then we spent time fucking, and even though the fucking was great in every way, we both decided we liked the talking better.

It was very unprofessional to get involved with one of the staff like that but Gene was a genuinely nice guy. He just wasn't my guy.

At the end of his probation period, I had to make a decision on whether to keep him on or fire his provocative ass. It was a no-brainer. He was good at his job. If I were honest I would have said he was better than Helen who rang in frequently for updates on how the old firm was getting on without her now that she was at home bored looking after her bouncing baby girl whom they'd named Traci.

The knock at my office door interrupted my daydreaming. Gene stuck his head in to say goodnight.

"Goodnight," I said, about to go back to a problem that had been bugging me all afternoon. I had a brainwave. We'd celebrate his becoming a permanent staff member, not that I needed an excuse for a party. "Gene? Are you free next Saturday for a barbecue at my place? I thought I might invite a few friends over."

"Barbecue sounds like fun."

"I'll leave the details on your desk with a list of people to phone to invite. I know it's not part of your duties…"

He waved away my concern.

"I'll see you tomorrow then. Night."

"Night, Buzz."

I sat at my desk and I suddenly realized how alone I was. I wanted to discuss my life and my options with someone and there was no one I could turn to. Cal had successfully alienated me from all my friends. Angrily, I shut down the computer and switched off the light. Even my home seemed more depressing than usual. I couldn't be bothered eating. I powered up my laptop and clicked through until I found the clip of me fucking Cal in the backyard. Unzipping my jeans, I hauled out my limp cock but no amount of prompting would get it hard, not even the sizzling images on the screen.

Slamming my fist down on the table, I took myself to bed where I slept only fitfully.

Saturday turned out warm and sunny, ideal for a pool party. Gene had invited people to bring their swimmers if it was fine and most people had accepted with alacrity. Gene and Artie helped me set up, Artie parading around in the smallest pair of Speedos I'd ever seen. They barely covered his dick and showed a lot more butt crack than would ever be allowed at the beach. I think he was trying to impress Gene.

I took Artie aside. "Is Cal coming?"

"Sorry, Buzz. I haven't seen Cal for ages. Not since he moved out of here."

I was puzzled. "I thought you two were going to keep seeing each other."

"So did I."

"Was it Zach?"

"Nah. I wouldn't have taken any notice of what he wanted. No, I rang a few times and left a message about catching up but Cal never rang back. I can take a hint."

"Thanks, Artie."

"It would be good to catch up with him again."

"Yeah, it would."

As the guests began arriving, I spent all my time welcoming them. I was disappointed when Izzy and Derek too turned up without Cal. They were hesitant about coming in but when I greeted them warmly, they relaxed a little, although they were thoroughly perplexed when I asked them about my son.

"We haven't seen Cal in weeks," Derek said.

Izzy was more aggressive. "He stopped being our friend because he said you didn't want him hanging around us anymore. We were bad influences. We only came today because we thought we might see him."

This was getting stranger by the minute.

"I haven't seen or spoken to him since he moved out of here. And I would never tell Cal to stop seeing you two, you're his best mates."

Derek turned on Izzy. "See, I told you. Sorry, Buzz. When Cal said what he did I wanted to ring you straight away because I thought there must be some mistake, but Izzy said to let it lie."

I was puzzled. "Surely you see him around the campus.

They looked at each other. This was going to get much worse before it got any better.

Izzy dropped his head in shame. "Cal dropped out. Said you didn't want him filling his head with all sorts of elitist bullshit. That he could come and work in your factory, do an honest day's toil. Learn from the factory floor up."

"Doesn't sound like anything I would ever say."

Derek agreed. "That's what I thought."

"Do you know where he's living?"

Izzy shrugged. "As we said. We thought he was here with you."

"Hang around after the party. We can catch up; maybe work out what's going on."

Vinnie and Roy, the two cops who had threatened to run me in as a Peeping Tom turned up, out of uniform as requested. They did look a bit out of place but I introduced them to a couple of friendly gay leather guys who were into rough trade, although not before I took Roy aside.

"Mate," I said. "Were you serious when you offered Cal your card?"

"You bet," Roy replied. "You and Cal are good guys in our opinion. Bit on the kinky side, I will admit, but good guys."

"Something strange is going on with Cal. He's sort of disappeared." I gave him a brief rundown including what Derek and Izzy had told me.

"Hey, count us in. We'd do anything for the kid."

Gene and Artie, although they seemed to have eyes only for each other, were also onside. I was grateful for anyone's support considering what transpired.

It was about an hour and a half into the party, the guests sufficiently lubricated, a few of them splashing about in the pool, others in groups inside the house and out chatting amiably, when Cal arrived with his entourage.

They didn't ring the front door bell, Cal still had a key. I was in the living room with Gene and Artie while Izzy and Derek were choosing music in the corner. Artie gasped at the change in Cal. He looked as if he hadn't slept in months, he was losing his muscle tone, and the bags under his eyes were the size of satchels. I'd invited everyone from that fateful gangbang night so it was no surprise Zach, Phil and Clive arrived together, dressed in identical leather. I just hadn't expected them to arrive with Cal in tow, covered immodestly by an ill-fitting bathing costume. Smug bastards. It was so obvious they were all out to humiliate me in front of my guests.

Clive stopped in front of me, yanking the chain attached to the slave collar around Cal's neck. It was a signal for him to drop to his knees. Being a slave, his eyes were downcast so I did not get a chance to gauge his reaction to seeing me again. As if to reinforce Cal's lowly position, Clive also had brought his pet German shepherd, Lucifer, on another lead. The parallel was obvious as both Cal and Lucifer sat worshipfully at Clive's feet.

"We got your invitation," Clive said.

"So I see. How are you Cal?" I asked.

There was no reply.

"You need permission."

"Permission to speak to my own son?'

Clive nodded his head. "And he needs permission to answer. Right Cal?

"Yes, sir." Cal said in a clear voice.

"I'll speak to my own son if I wish. I don't need your permission."

"You're right," Clive said. "But I can sure as fuck punish Cal if you do." So saying he pushed my son down on all fours to reveal the crimson stripes across his back, some of the wounds still slightly bleeding. Cal flinched as Clive ran his hand across the injuries.

"You bastard…" I clenched my fist but Gene grabbed my hand, holding it tightly.

Clive didn't miss the interaction. He addressed Gene. "That's right, don't let your boyfriend lose his cool. Cal wants to be like this, it appeals to his submissive nature. It's all of his own free will. Isn't it slave?"

"Yes, sir."

"See he wants to be the best slave there is but he's a long way from perfect yet. Stubborn. Headstrong. Has to be punished to remind him of his place."

There was no point arguing.

Clive examined Gene carefully. "Mmm, I like your new boyfriend. Very cute. What did you say his name was?" Clive asked.

In that moment Cal looked up and I saw distress in his eyes, probably believing I had replaced him in my affections already. Zach saw the movement as well and brought the riding crop he carried down on Cal's back. Cal screamed, shrinking in on himself in case there were more blows to follow. I could not show any emotion and it was killing me inside.

"Gene's not…"

Gene squeezed my fingers tighter, I presumed warning me not to tell him we weren't lovers.

I corrected myself. "Yes, his name is Gene."

I felt Artie tense behind me.

Clive turned to Zach and Phil. "Tasty little dish. Maybe we'll try him next. Cal's just about all clapped out now. His ass is as wide as a canyon. I suppose we should have taken better care of him but our mates do like a good ass to fuck on a drunken weekend gangbang. And Cal fits the bill nicely. Or he did. So how about it, Gene?"

Clive put a finger under Gene's chin, lifting it as if examining a race horse or some other piece of property. I just hoped Artie would keep his cool. I could feel him about to go to Gene's defense, but in the end he didn't have to. Clive tried harder to push our buttons by running his finger along Gene's lips. He was surprised when Gene opened his mouth and licked the finger, encouraging him to insert it in his mouth. He was even more surprised when Gene began to suck on the finger as if in submission to a superior man. Then Gene's hand shot out grasping Clive's wrist. He struggled but Gene chomped down on the finger causing Clive to cry out in pain. When he extracted his finger, Clive discovered a nasty ring of teeth marks around it.

With a steady voice, Gene said, "You didn't ask my permission." Clive attempted to turn the tables but no one was buying it. "I like a guy with spunk. You'll be a pleasure to break. And break you I will my little filly." To reinforce his superiority, and I suppose to show he was not afraid, Clive smoothed Gene's cheek with the back of his hand. He was smart enough to watch out for the punishing teeth or even a fist. He wasn't smart enough to watch for Gene's knee barreling into his balls.

Clive bent over double in pain and even Zach and Phil flinched. Clive was kneeling in pain, gasping for breath, as his back-up went to help him stand. He waved them away. He would do it on his own. Hoisting himself to his feet, his face flushed purple, Clive grabbed the crop, whipping it three times across poor Cal's back. Cal whimpered.

Gene held my hand tightly.

Gene stood up to him. "If that's meant to scare me, you're doing a miserable job of it. You'll never get me down on my knees in front of you. And if you think I care what you do to that stupid slut, think again." Clive brought the riding crop down on Cal even harder. "By the looks of the poor sod, he'll be dead by Christmas. If you don't do it, then the booze, the drugs or the fucking will get him. Go ahead, put him out of his misery."

"What do you want Clive?" I asked, in case he was tempted to do just that.

"I thought we were mates. We just came to enjoy the party. Plus we brought you a bit of entertainment. I'm sure you'll enjoy it. Has a little audience participation which I'm sure you'll love."

"And if I refuse to participate?"

Clive brought the crop down hard on Cal's back again without even looking at him. I couldn't bring myself to look either.

His voice taking on an evil sibilant quality that made my flesh crawl, Clive got right into my face, "Don't ever again, ever, tell me who I can and cannot fuck! I don't care if it's your son, your wife, your father. Nobody, but nobody, tells me who I can have on the end of my cock. As for that feeble threat about losing your friendship, what made you think I wanted it in the first place?"

"Is that what this is all about?"

"And because your son is an arrogant little shit. I don't forget easily. I still remember what he was like when he was here last. That smirking attitude when he put us all down. Well, look who's down now. Thought he was so superior and now all he is is a worthless cum dump. Come on, let's join the party."

Clive dragged Cal and Lucifer out into the pool area where a few old hands greeted them cheerfully. Phil and Zach looked to be in their element. We held back, Derek and Izzy shocked at the condition of their friend, Artie close to tears and ready to tear the three of them apart with his bare hands. Gene's face had turned the color of ash. I was devastated at what they'd done to my son.

Roy and Vinnie came looking for us.

"What the fuck have they done to Cal?" Roy asked. "He looks half dead."

Derek explained the situation briefly.

"There must be something we can book them on," Vinnie said.

"They've got Cal so brain washed and scared he'll say it's all his free choice. There's no coercion involved."

"Bullshit," Roy spat.

Gene was the voice of doom. "They've got something really nasty cooked up for you Buzz. I can feel it. Something public and very humiliating. Probably for both of you."

"Whatever they dish up, I can take. I don't know about Cal."

"You don't have to get involved, Buzz," Roy said.

"Did you see Cal's back? They're threatening that if I don't co-operate, Cal will be punished. Punished severely. I don't know if he could take much more."

"Give me their names," Roy said. "Vinnie will ring them through and see if we've got anything we can pin on the bastards or, at least, slow them down."

There was the sound of applause outside just before Phil stuck his head round the door. "Get your butts outside gentlemen. The show is about to start."

Clive had organized the outdoor area so people were standing, squatting, sitting in plastic sun chairs, leaning against the buffet tables, even sitting on the tiles, with a view of a central area where Cal was kneeling. I stood at the back trembling with anger.

Clive looked like he'd won the lottery. "Gents, we're all friends here. In fact most of you," he looked around the crowd, "if not all of you were here on that famous night when we all fucked Buzz's little slut boy here with total disregard for Buzz's paternal feelings."

The crowd murmured mutinously not wanting that secret revealed, a few panicked looks were aimed in my direction.

"Yes, Buzz, you are the last to know that all your so-called friends rammed their pricks in Cal's boy cunt or his mouth. Some of them more than once. What does that tell you about the regard your friends hold you in, eh? Sorry you had to find out your boy is a glutton for cock this way. Oh wait, no I'm not."

"You're wasting your breath, Clive. I know all about the party. I was here when it happened. I saw the whole thing." I gave a few examples of things I'd witnessed. I watched as a number of people cringed and a few crept away in the dark.

"No matter," Clive said cheerfully. "So you already know what a cock slut your boy is. But I bet the people here tonight don't know that you fucked your son up the ass in a shithouse at the airport. And that it fuckin' turned you on!"

I tried to keep my voice as calm as possible. "That's before I knew he was my son. I hadn't seen him in six or seven years. He'd changed."

"Yeah. He's changed from a fag hater to a fag slut." Clive clicked his fingers and Cal stripped off his flimsy swimming costume and lay on one of the low tables set up for his impromptu performance. He spread his legs wide like a contortionist so his sweet ass was center stage. There was a large black silicone plug blocking his hole.

We watched in fascinated horror as Lucifer padded over to Cal and began lapping at his vulnerable ass and his balls. There were snickers from the crowd when they noticed Lucifer's cock expanding.

Clive ignored the fuss. "Cal was supposed to go to university this year but we convinced him that his ass was too precious to squander on hard classroom seats and benches. We convinced him by regularly fucking that cute twink ass until it was filled to overflowing with slimy man juice. In fact, before we came to the party today, Zach, Phil and I had the immense pleasure, along with five or six of our mates, I forget exactly how many it was…"

"Six," Phil called

"Six, of depositing our loads in that hot ass. It may not be as tight as it once was but who is?"

A number of the guests laughed.

"And where's the man whose sperm created this lovely young lad. Come over here Buzz. Take a bow. You must be so proud."

I walked over and stood near Cal, wondering what on earth I could do to help him. Had I known, it would have been better to concentrate on what I could do to help me.

"Buzz, please lie down beneath your sweet boy's ass. We don't want you to miss a trick."

When I looked confused, Phil dragged Lucifer away, securing him to the back fence, while Zach rough-housed me into position lying face up on the tiles beneath Cal's butthole. I had a fair idea of what was coming but I didn't give Clive enough credit for his sheer perversity. I was only half right.

"Gentlemen, please be prepared to be impressed. Cal's dad will now have a ringside view and a ringside tasting of all that lovely spooge we dumped in his son's toxic ass earlier today." His voice rising like an old-fashioned carnival spruiker, he announced, "I give you Cal's gape year."

I had to give him credit for theatricality because he timed it perfectly, yanking the butt plug from Cal's ass as he uttered the words 'gape year.' My admiration was short lived because once the plug was pulled wads of spooge cascaded from the hitherto dammed hole straight onto my face.

Clive sounded pleased, "Open up, Buzz."

I knew if I baulked at any of this, Cal would cop another severe beating. No matter how revolted I was at having to drink Zach and Phil and Clive's disloyal spunk, I had to go through with it. I glanced about the crowd as best I could as my face became slimier and noticed some guys were turned on by the display. To my horror I realized my cock had been as hard as granite since Cal had spread his legs and that with swallowing the waterfall of cum, I was in serious danger of blowing my own load.

"Show the audience your hole, Cal."

"Yes, sir!" he answered before anchoring his fingers on either side of his hole to flatten his cheeks to give people a better view of his gaping raw asshole. A late evacuation of cum plopped onto my forehead. His ass seemed wide enough for him to have given birth.

"I know most of you gents partook of Cal's tight little hole last time, but in honor of Cal's gape year he's inviting you to have another go. It may be sloppy, it may not be quite as snug as last time, but what the hell, it's free. And you'll have the added satisfaction of knowing his dad has a front-row seat as your long hard prick pounds his son's guts. After your cum has fermented inside our bottom boy, his dad will have the unmitigated pleasure of swallowing it all down. Now, who wants a go? I know, how about Buzz's new boyfriend. Wouldn't it be a treat to watch dad's new boyfriend fuck his son?"

There was an excited murmur. Gene stepped forward, obviously afraid Cal would cop a beating if he didn't, but rather than appear the reluctant groom, Gene stood proudly, stripped his clothes off as if Clive's request was nothing, and advanced on Cal's butt, his cock already hard.

"Glad to oblige," Gene boasted. "The little cunt has been nothing but trouble since the day he arrived. It'll be a real pleasure to fuck him into oblivion."

Just above my face, I watched as Gene's beautiful thick cock slid its way into Cal's guts. I watched fascinated and as horny as hell at the best butt fuck Cal was ever likely to receive. I learned later Gene leaned into Cal until they almost went into a lip lock. Cal stared into his eyes and something passed between them. After he'd blown his load, Gene pulled out, taking the opportunity to look down at me and whisper encouragingly, "Hang in there."

For close to two hours, I lay watching Cal's ass repeatedly buggered. Yes, they gave him rest breaks so his legs would not cramp but I didn't move. I watched small cocks, big cocks, cut cocks, uncut cocks, rough cocks, thick cocks, all plow his raw hole as they shot their spunk deep inside him, a lot of it oozing into my mouth. There was no shirking my humiliation. I had to lie there and take it, my heart bleeding for my poor battered boy. I spent the time attempting to come to terms with my feelings for Cal. On the one hand he's my son, on the other he's a hot fuck. Do I love him as one or the other? Or both?

Why am I so turned on watching cock after cock ram into his pliant ass? Why do I want to be one of the guys gangbanging him? Is Cal really a cock whore or is it all just a ruse to make me jealous, to make me play attention to him? Why does it excite me to watch Clive, my treacherous best mate, run Cal's ass ragged? And why am I aching to see those human shits Phil and Zach, balls dangling close to my face, plunging their cocks inside my sweet son.

I was disgusted with myself that my cock remained hard for the whole two hours I was forced to lie on the tiles, even after I had twice blown a load.

Long after his ass could take no more and Cal whimpered 'enough' so quietly that only I heard him, he was lifted to sit on my face and empty the slime in his bowels directly into my mouth. I swallowed as best I could but there was so much it covered my face and my hair. When I felt the last of it and sensed that Cal had been carried off, I wiped my eyes. Derek and Izzy helped me to the kitchen where I spewed what seemed like a bucketful of cock snot into the sink. Even as I did so, perversely I regretted I couldn't keep it all down. I wiped my face enough to get upstairs and shower because I knew my friends would be waiting for me in the living room, the other partygoers having left earlier or as soon as Cal was taken away.

The hot water cleared the slime from my face and hair, although I knew I'd have bloodshot eyes tomorrow where the sperm had got into them. My body ached from lying on the cold hard tiles but that pain was insignificant in comparison to what Cal was enduring. Did I feel humiliated? Not at all, as it transpires. Maybe I'm missing something in my DNA? I really wanted to talk to someone about my reactions. There was only one person I knew would understand but he was not among the men downstairs waiting to discuss strategy with me. Sure they were supportive, and sure they'd be front-line soldiers in our forthcoming intervention to get Cal back before any more harm could be done, but I thought of Lucifer and shuddered.

The only person who would really understand my conflicting feelings was the very person we were planning to rescue.

Cal, my son.

SON & GAMES

Cal was screaming for it. Even though the sound was crap I could hear every word as he begged the overweight bozo plowing his butt to 'ram my fuckin' sleazy asshole until I bleed. Make me your whore. Fill my boy cunt with your spunk till it runs down my leg.'

The scene sickened me because my handsome boy was copping the fuck of his life from a butt ugly sleazebag who was sweating like Niagara Falls as he slammed his brutal prick into my son's guts. What's more, I could tell Cal wasn't acting. He was loving every second of this ass battering. The ultimate humiliation was that all three of us watching the video were so turned on we had to keep adjusting the tent in our trousers to hide our treachery.

"I think that's enough," Vinnie said as he squeezed his cock in an effort to hide it from me. "You get the idea anyway. That's the main point."

Roy turned on the lights careful to keep his back to us so we couldn't see the outline of his erection in his cop pants. At least he and Vinnie had an excuse; we'd just been watching a good half hour of the most graphic fuck footage imaginable, a video of my son being buggered into oblivion by middle-aged scum in a dismal motel room. I should have been revolted by what I'd seen and I was. But for all the wrong reasons. His sex partners were gross and selfish – and I wished they were me.

Ever since Cal had come back into my life I'd struggled with my attraction to him. Like many a callous youth who had little regard for social niceties, content only with the pursuit of his own satisfaction, he'd willingly succumbed to the illicit passion we had for each other. He had been quite content to settle down in a relationship with his dad.

I'm afraid my mind couldn't come to grips with that idea even while my body screamed that was exactly what it wanted. The video footage brought that home to me with a clarity that had been missing from my life over the past few weeks.

"Where did you get it?" I asked, my voice almost breaking with stress. "How old is it?"

Vinnie looked as if he'd rather rip out his tongue than answer my questions. He and Roy had become good friends since we'd met in less than ideal circumstances when they'd caught me peeping on my son through my living room window. They genuinely liked Cal and were as distressed by his downward spiral as I was.

"The Drug Squad boys keep us in the loop. Besides they owe us big time."

Roy filled me in. "The motel's on the interstate on the outskirts of town. Well known venue for hookers and hustlers to ply their trade. Drug Squad are staking it out for a big deal that's going down. They've got all the rooms wired, taking no chances. When they found out we were looking for Cal they showed us some of the...um... highlights they captured."

"There's more?"

"Fuckin' hours of it," Vinnie said with a touch of awe.

"We just showed you the best bits," Roy said with just a little too much pleasure.

"What exactly is the Drug Squad doing about it?"

Vinnie was obviously embarrassed. "Not exactly their jurisdiction. They don't want to blow their cover."

I was disgusted. "Yeah, I get it. They don't want to get involved."

Roy couldn't help shooting his mouth off. "I wouldn't say that," he smirked. "That last guy you saw on the video is Con, one of the Drug Squad boys. Said he got so turned on monitoring the room he waited until the last john left then went in to get a taste of boy cunt for himself."

Vinnie kicked him and glanced warily at the CCTV camera set into the wall at ceiling height.

I was down at police headquarters. It was three weeks since Cal had turned up at my party with his three 'masters' and put on a demonstration of such depravity that his reputation had been enhanced. Cal's was the go-to-ass in the town if you wanted a taste of the angels. Or so it was said. I'd tasted and I wanted more. I wasn't the only one.

After the party Cal had slipped under the radar. I hadn't been able to track him down. Nor had his closest mates Derek and Izzy. I'd heard rumors of behavior so gross it was difficult to believe they hadn't been exaggerated just to give me emotional dyspepsia. Whoever started the tales of depravity obviously knew the stories would get back to me.

I'd gone in search of Cal but had never found him. His new friends obviously kept him well hidden only bringing him out for the maximum humiliation for me when the buzz on the street got spread about his anal prowess. I knew something was brewing. Something big. It would not be good news for me. It would be even worse for Cal, of that I was sure.

So were Vinnie and Roy, which is why they were helping me out in every way possible. They'd been at the party where my erstwhile friends Phil, Clive and Zach threw Cal to the horny crowd, making me witness to my son's sexual humiliation by my closest personal friends, Gene, Artie, Izzy and Derek. Phil had warned of dire retribution if they didn't join the party at Cal's back entrance.

Once I'd washed up after swallowing not only my pride but the contents of Cal's fetid fucked ass including the spooge slime of my worst enemies as well as my best friends only to discover my cock was embarrassingly hard, a group of us held an emergency meeting.

Roy and Vinnie, the two cops, Derek and Izzy, Cal's two best friends from university, plus my workers, Gene and Artie, joined me for a brainstorming session. The cops were more than willing to 'borrow' a few kilos from their Drug Squad mates to stitch up the treacherous trio who were responsible for Cal's transformation and I saw no reason not to fight dirty. Artie didn't look convinced but kept mum in the face of overwhelming approval. Apart from that idea, there seemed little we could do but keep in contact and meet again in three days.

Phil, Zach and Clive played it very low key after their attempt at gross humiliation at my party obviously saving their next move for something spectacular. I had already assumed they were regular users and abusers of Cal's sweet asshole and insatiable mouth, as well as sharing same with others on a regular basis. The video footage Roy and Vinnie showed me confirmed those worst suspicions. I felt so helpless especially in view of Cal's complicity in his own depravity.

I blamed myself. If I'd been more amenable to Cal's needs and my own desires I would have given the finger to conventional morality and taken him to my bed as my lover. But there were other considerations: the legal aspects not least of all. Plus there was his antagonistic mother and his step-father who would take any opportunity to separate the two of us without the added ammunition that a charge of incest would bring.

Sleep came to me rarely and when it did it was filled with hideous nightmares in which Cal berated me for my lack of courage and for his subsequent descent into hell before giving himself to my enemies in the most lascivious and disgusting manner possible. The dreams usually culminated in my ejaculation into the sheets as I watched Cal embrace his own downfall. If reality was even half as explicit as my sleep fantasies then my son was doomed.

I was a zombie at work so I was lucky that Artie and Gene kept the company on a steady course. They coaxed me to sign papers, guiding me expertly through the salient points of any contracts, offering commiseration and a friendly ear when I needed it. Their strength kept me, and the company, afloat, giving me time to pass through the guilt phase of my depression to emerge about ten days later determined to win back my son. I would use every means at my disposal. I was ready to kick major ass, to beg Cal's forgiveness, to throw caution to the wind. If necessary, I would also throw the tattered remains of conventional morality to the winds as well.

It was agony waiting those three weeks until we had concrete news of Cal. Had it not been for the Drug Squad stake-out, I doubt we would have had any information about my son at all. I was grateful to see that he was still alive because, unspoken among our group, was the concern that his poor body could not stand too much of the punishment being meted out to him by the three sleaze bags who now claimed him as their slave. It was a given that we believed his outrageous behavior was as a result of a dependence on drugs. I had less reason to believe that than most as I'd seen Cal's callous slutty conduct when he was stone cold sober of both alcohol and addictive medicinal substances.

But slutty behavior was very different to the insatiable monster he'd become. Even at his worst, when he lived with me, he was still concerned about his education and his future. Right now it looked as if his near future could be contained in a pine box six feet beneath the earth.

I found that one of the best ways to still my concern for Cal's safety and to clear my mind was the gym. Lifting weights, crunches, step classes, anything to keep me occupied. It struck me as ironic that while Cal's looks and his musculature were being ravaged by his own actions I was building myself up into one of the hottest studs around. Perhaps, subconsciously, I believed that one look at the new me would be enough to get him to revert to the old Cal. It was a forlorn hope if I did.

It was on my way to one of my aggressive workouts, about four weeks after his disappearance, that I heard from him. If it was really him and not one of his so-called 'masters.' I would have called them much worse names. My phone vibrated. I flipped it quickly to Open Message when the screen acknowledged that it had come from Cal's phone. I wasn't dumb enough to think it was necessarily from him.

"Hi dad," the message read. "If u want 2 c the new me meet me at..."

My heart skipped excitedly at the opening of the message. For an instant I believed that Cal had escaped the insidious clutches of his tormentors and started afresh. It was short-lived. The meeting place was a park, notorious for the all-male activity in the bushes and in the squat brick male toilet. It could be a trap but to what purpose I had no idea. Maybe Cal had changed. I had to keep the appointment, no matter the consequences but I rang Artie and Gene to let them know my plans. They both volunteered to come with me but this was something I needed to do alone. To cover my back, I rang Roy and told him what had gone down. He and Vinnie were otherwise engaged with family commitments and couldn't protect me but Roy offered to send Sam along as back-up.

"You met him at the station," he said.

I remembered the guy. Chubby build, friendly enough, face like a squashed mango because of too many street fights, taciturn. He'd scare the bejesus out of anyone who came across him in the dark.

"He lives near the park. I'll get him to take a look around ten, that was the meeting time right?"

"Appreciate it, Roy. It's mainly in case those bastards are up to something. Not that I believe for a moment they'd do me any real physical harm."

I did genuinely believe that. They'd stayed just the right side of the law so far and I didn't think any of them would be likely to jeopardize their family or their future over me. It's not like I'd ever done anything to them except try to deny them access to Cal's ass. They'd managed anyway. They believed they'd humiliated me in front of my friends and in Cal's opinion so what more could they possibly want?

I left my car in a side street to walk the last block to the designated meeting place. It was a large park, more bush than landscaped lawns and gardens giving ample cover to any clandestine activity including violence. A few men smoked, lounging about on the benches dotting the pathway that meandered through the thickets, their legs spread wide in open invitation.

My T-shirt was tight around my honed torso and my jeans hugged my substantial package and my sculpted ass so that a number of invitations were issued by the clasp of a hand over groin or the opening wider of legs and the flick of a tongue. All manner of delights were promised and if my mission were not so serious I would have succumbed to any of the good-looking men who ogled me. I suppose the way I appraised those men, searching for Cal or one of my enemies, gave some of them the wrong idea and one or two followed at a distance. I lost them when I sped up my circumlocution of the park.

No sign of Cal anywhere. That left only the place my brain told me I should have explored initially. But I was an optimist, I'd hoped for the best. Now it was obvious even to me that the New Cal was not a change for the better.

Scraping my shoes on the cement paving outside the entrance to the men's toilet, the universal warning sign to those inside, I entered slowly in order to accustom my eyes to the dark as someone had thoughtfully smashed the overhead lights inside. The vandals though had left one light attached to the wall above the urinal which gave off an eerie glow that was just enough to see dimly.

Once inside the toilet proper there were three mirrors on the wall above three identical wash basins immediately upon entry. A paper towel dispenser that looked as if it had not been filled since the Renaissance waited forlornly to one side. Along one wall there were four cubicles with wooden doors that reached almost to the floor. Only one seemed to be in use. A quick glance confirmed that rather large glory holes had been cut or drilled into the dividing walls. Large enough to share a picnic lunch let alone a cock or two.

The urinal, one of those old-fashioned aluminum troughs, ran along the wall opposite the cubicles and it was here that a small number of men congregated probably taking a piss or else fumbling with each other's cock. I leaned against one of the basins until my eyes were fully accustomed to the gloom. None of the three men with their backs to me was Cal which meant he had to be in the cubicle, provided of course this wasn't a set-up.

I was about to enter the vacant cubicle next to the occupied stall when one of the men at the urinal grunted, stepped back, shook his cock and moved away to zip up leaving a space. I was horrified to see Cal kneeling in the trough with his mouth suckling one of the remaining men's pricks seemingly oblivious to the fact he was kneeling in piss and who knew what else. He was stark naked, his tumescent cock clamped in perpetual erection by a metal cock ring around his prick and his balls.

He seemed to have the use of only one hand and it wasn't until the second man moved closer for his turn at

Cal's mouth that I noticed the other arm was handcuffed to the metal pipes that flushed the toilet. He was trapped, there was no escape. As the second man zipped up and left, the light caught Cal's body for an instant before the remaining man pushed his dick in Cal's waiting mouth.

Cal's naked body shone with streaks of slime over his chest and in his hair. But it was his face that was remarkable. It was a mess of slimy running spunk. He had obviously been locked in position for a very long time with men taking advantage of his inability to escape to unload on his face and down his throat. I wondered how many had tagged his ass.

The guy fucking Cal's face had his head in a vise-like grip so that he was unable to move. I stripped off my T and jeans, milking my prick as I watched the action.

"Suck it, pussy boy. Suck all the spunk out of my cock," the guy was moaning. "Drain my balls. Swallow my spicy cum."

He saw me watching him and leaned over to slap Cal's ass. "Stand up, slut. Bend over."

Cal did as commanded and his beautiful butthole was an open invitation to anyone who wanted entry. My son still had his mouth attached to the guy's cock so he hadn't noticed I was there. He obviously had no concept of the time. He probably had no idea I had even been invited. This was another trick of the trio to break me. They'd need to try much harder than this. I was buzzing watching Cal suck cock. If I stopped to consider my excitement it had to do with the fact it was my son, the guy I loved in a manner I shouldn't, who was sucking cock like a sex pig that turned me on. So Cal was a slut. Fuck, that was a plus. That he was cuffed naked in a public toilet for anyone to use...how hot was that?

That he was kneeling in rancid old piss, his face covered with man slime, his stomach full of ball juice and his ass raped raw...life didn't get much better than that.

His face fucker grunted and spat out a few more expletives as I fingered Cal's sloppy butthole, feeling the mingled spooge from who knew how many hot man cocks that had left their mark in his gut. In a few minutes I'd leave mine there as well.

The other guy pulled out, squeezing the last pearl of juice from his slit so Cal could lick it off, then zipped up and left the building.

"On your back," I commanded.

Cal looked up in surprise at my voice. "Dad?"

"Hi, Cal. How's my son slut?"

"What do you care?" he sulked.

"I care enough that I'm gonna fuck your spooge-filled cunt hole until I blow the biggest load you'll get tonight. I'm gonna breed my son's hole with my daddy spunk. You like that idea, son?"

I snarled at him. This was a grudge fuck, it wasn't meant to be pleasant. As he lay on the edge of the stinking urinal, I lifted his legs, parted his cheeks and rammed my cock inside without any prep. There was little friction, he must have played host to a dozen or more men to be this loose and sloppy. It was like fucking warm custard. I loved it.

"Sloppy cunt, son. Mmmmm, feel your dad's cock inside you. Forbidden cock, son. Law says you can't have this cock but we both know you need it and you need it bad. Makes you complete. You'll never be able to break the connection no matter how hard you try. You're mine, boy. Always will be."

I saw the sadness in Cal's eyes as he mouthed the word 'Sorry' just seconds before I felt the blow to the back of my head and I sank into the darkness. I don't know how long passed before I had the overwhelming feeling I was drowning. I heard voices. "Shit, you mean these two guys are father and son?"

Somewhere a familiar voice was agreeing but I was concentrating on not taking more foul water into my nose and mouth. My head ached, my ass hurt, my eyes were stinging. As I regained consciousness I remembered where I had been ambushed. If the taste in my mouth was anything to go by I was still in the same place.

"If you don't let his face up, he'll drown," that familiar voice said.

The grip relaxed and I pulled my head up gasping for breath. The sudden movement sent pain behind my eyes right to my brain. It was like a savage blow to the solar plexus. My face had been submerged in the urinal and I gagged as the smell got into my throat. Blinking to focus my eyes, I was being hammered doggy style facing the urinal. By the feel of spooge oozing out my ass my rapist was not the first to have his cock in me that night. To my side, Cal was on his back taking a fat slob of a man in his butt. Cal was begging for it, egging the gross slug to spew a load into his guts. It wasn't play acting, it was for real.

So this was the new Cal someone had wanted me to see. Did I love him any the less for his disgusting behavior? Not a bit of it. It might seem strange to many that I wasn't repulsed by what I was seeing and that my own son had lured me into the trap. It had opened my eyes to what I'd always wanted. I suspect it had done much the same to Cal.

The gross pig banging Cal's butt oinked as his load squirted, his body convulsing until every ounce of his spooge was inside my son. He pulled out, Cal's ass expelling a load of spunk he was so full of ball snot. I didn't know what Zach intended, for it was his voice that eventually registered in my fuzzy brain but I knew we were safe. Roy had one of his cop mates on the job and any minute now there'd be sirens and flashing lights and handcuffs on my nemesis.

I struggled because, just like Cal, I was handcuffed to the flush pipes by one arm.

"These two fuckin' whores could make a fortune as a double act," the guy who'd just dumped in my ass commented. He patted my head like I was a good dog and I wanted to knock him into the middle of next week.

My ass was on fire but that didn't prevent the next fucker from sliding his prick inside me to begin banging away, puffing his exertion over my back. I looked across to Cal whose eyes were glazed over, hardly focusing any more on the pummeling his body was enduring.

"Not long now, buddy," I whispered although I knew he wouldn't hear me. But if I thought it would give me extra courage I was wrong. Cal's next rider stepped up, slapping his ass to wake him from his sexual stupor. I couldn't believe my eyes when I saw Sam, the cop who was supposed to look out for me, slip his large cut cock into Cal's spooge hole. I wanted to scream especially as Sam smiled when he saw me watching him, winking as he rode my boy's ass rough enough to get him begging again.

If I got out of this alive, I'd kill the cunt.

I lost count of the men who dumped in my mouth and my ass, gritting my teeth as I planned my revenge against not only the three men who had destroyed Cal but also Sam who let them get away with it. He'd left after slapping Cal about the face as he roared his triumphant orgasm into Cal's butt. He pulled out, patting Cal on the ass and said, "I hope we can do this again."

Over my dead body.

I heard him talking to Zach but they must have taken the conversation outside. I don't know how many minutes later it was when I heard a siren and Sam race back in and shout, "Scatter, the cops are coming!"

There was an air of panic as guys zipped up and ran for their lives. Zach had Cal out of his cuffs in record time and hoisted him over his shoulder.

"Hey, what about me?" I yelled as he headed for the exit.

I heard a snicker as he disappeared.

I swore vehemently. Thwarted again and only a sore ass and a phlegmy throat to show for it. Maybe a bit of concussion. How was I going to explain this to the police?

It didn't look as if I was going to have to explain anything for Sam swaggered back into the shithouse. On his own. My blood pressure went through the roof as I imagined as many terrible ways of disposing of him as I could.

"Bastard!" I spat.

He handed me a bottle of water which I guzzled in an effort to clear my throat, pouring the remainder over my hair and face to get rid of the smell of piss and cum. Sam tried a number of keys in the handcuffs until they sprang open.

"Can you stand up?" he said.

I was wobbly but managed to stay upright by leaning one hand against the wall. I'd have to bide my time before I launched an attack. Sam wrapped me in a blanket to cover my nakedness then retrieved my clothes, sodden and reeking, from one of the cubicles before helping me hobble to his car.

"You drive here?" he asked as he buckled me into the front seat of his vehicle.

I told him where I'd parked the car. He fumbled through my trousers until he found the keys. He was gone only a few minutes before he returned and parked my car behind his own.

I leaned out the open door of his vehicle to puke my guts out in the gutter. Sam wiped my face with a tissue. I must have fallen asleep because I don't remember anything until I felt myself being manhandled again and found myself in the passenger's seat of my own car.

The following few hours were a blur although I remembered being helped into my own home and being lowered into a hot bath which sucked all the pain out of my aching muscles and my throbbing hole. Then I slept. It was the muffled sound of voices that woke me. Staggering out of bed, I found the dressing gown I'd bought when I'd heard the news Cal was coming to stay, wrapping myself in its comfortable familiarity.

All my friends were deep in conversation when I made my unscheduled appearance. Artie was up out of his seat when he saw me, helping me to one of the lounge chairs. There was a lot of genuine concern as they fussed over me. My only response was to threaten Sam with an incredibly painful torture and death.

"Take it easy," Roy said. "Now is not the time to go into details but there was a reason for what he did. Just accept that for the moment because he's got us the best lead we're likely to get on how to rescue Cal and how to nail the bastards who did this to you."

"Okay," I replied although I remained unconvinced.

Roy sighed. "Sam gained Zach's trust enough by what he did and by telling a few porkies about his contacts and his influence with the police in the town to get an invite."

"To what?" I asked.

"I don't know how to tell you this, except to say that if Sam here hadn't fucked Cal then he never would have got the information he did."

"So tell me already."

"Zach, Phil and Clive intend to raise big money by putting on a show out at that biker bar on the city limits. The main attraction will be Cal." Roy paused. He took a deep breath before he went on. "His co-star will be Lucifer."

I remembered the ferocious German shepherd the gang had brought to the party. I shuddered.

"When he's finished tearing up Cal's ass then anyone in the bar who wants a go can take a turn. Part of the price of admission. At the end of the night if Cal hasn't been fucked to hell and back, there's to be an auction. Cal will go to the highest bidder to do what he wants."

"We can't fuckin' let that happen." I held back tears at the thought of it.

"Vinnie's been in touch with the drug boys and between us we reckon we've got a plan."

It was a good plan as far as it went but I wasn't convinced it went far enough. What did I know? Well, I knew that no one had come up with anything better and that if this worked then I would have Cal back, provided he wanted to be back, and the three bastards would be out of circulation for some considerable time.

Sam had taken the time to explain that he'd only fucked Cal under duress. He had conned Zach and was about to reel him in when Zach wanted some sort of proof about Sam's bona fides. He did the only thing he could. He gritted his teeth and slipped his hitherto straight cock into Cal's buggered hole cursing him as a slut and the spawn of Satan. Sheepishly, he admitted he got turned on half way through the fuck and wasn't acting any more.

I smiled. Yeah, Cal had that sort of power in his ass.

With the help of police prosthetic artists I was unrecognizable by the time Sam and I drove out to the party. He had a VIP pass so there were no stringent searches or up-close inspections and we slipped inside to disappear amongst the boisterous crowd. The plan was to wait until the last minute to ensure the cops could ensnare the whole mob with enough evidence to put them behind bars, and set Cal free. I was nervous about it; the intervention needed split second timing.

Once all the doors to the bar were closed and security stationed outside, the cops would wait for the signal via Sam's mobile phone. Thank god, we were all allowed to bring our phones in order that we could take pics or footage of the night's entertainment. With luck, it wouldn't get to that point.

I was a nervous wreck, unable to sit still or stand in one spot. I knew I was driving Sam crazy so I moved aside to let him concentrate on surveillance. It was probably a mistake because I ran straight into Clive who was doing the rounds to ensure everyone was having a good time. He stared at me with a puzzled look as if to try to place me. He shook his head and I saluted him with my drink, muttering "Great party."

He smiled. "Thanks. It's gonna get even better. Enjoy."

I breathed easier as he pushed his way through the crowds.

The entertainment was on late and by the time it was due to begin I'd had rather more than I intended. I was pissed just enough that I was feeling no pain. Phil appeared on the makeshift stage that had been set up in one corner of the bar to call for quiet and to explain about the night's entertainment to whoops of appreciation. When he announced that Cal would take on all comers there was an awed hush as people looked around the numbers in the bar. It didn't take a mathematician to calculate Cal was in deep shit.

My boy was brought out on stage naked to wild cheers and much lascivious banter. He waved his appreciation of the crowd but I could see even at my distance from the stage that he was drug fucked. He assumed the position, lying face down over a small table that had been made comfortable with cushions covered by a blanket. Zach greased his asshole slipping three fingers in until Cal was practically begging to be fucked.

When Clive walked on stage with Lucifer on his leash the crowd erupted. The dog was startled for a moment but Clive calmed the animal leading him over to Cal, spread-eagled and ready. I looked over to Sam whose attention was so taken by the scene unfolding on stage he had not texted to his colleagues outside.

I understood because I was hard as stone in my trousers half hoping/half dreading.

As Clive encouraged Lucifer, the audience was so quiet I could hear my heart beating in my ears. The whole world seemed to stop except for the impending depravity on stage. I was in a sort of trance as I watched, at least until there was a roar of approval from the crowd and I came out of my funk. Shit! Where was the back-up? I elbowed Sam in the ribs. He almost dropped his phone but it brought him back to reality, his thumbs working overtime as he sent off the signal to the cops surrounding the building.

Because the crowd was now hushed in awe, everyone heard the sound of sledgehammers against the doors. There was a yell of 'Cops' which caused panic and I was swept up in the wave of bodies attempting to find an escape route. The last I saw of Sam was him punching his way through the crowd toward Cal on the stage. I followed as best I could, pushing and shoving people out of my way. I had no idea where Zach, Phil and Clive had got to but I could hear Lucifer barking in terror from the stage.

The crush of bodies was one of the most frightening things I've ever experienced. People fell to the floor while others trod over them in their desperation to escape. It was a miracle no one was killed. And then as quickly as it began, it was all over. I was by Cal's side on the stage but he was so out of it he had no idea what was happening.

Roy made his way over with the grin of success plastered across his face.

"The Drugs boys are very happy," he said. "Unfortunately, Phil got away but the other two are in the paddy wagon on the way to the station. How's Cal?"

"He doesn't look too good," I said.

Roy summoned one of the young cops who was rounding up the stragglers.

"We need to get this guy to a hospital but he needs a guard twenty-four/seven. Think you can handle that?"

"Yes, sir."

"I'd take you myself," Roy explained, "but I have to write up the report on all this because the shit is really going to hit the fan once it gets out."

I understood.

As I carried Cal toward the exit, following the young cop who was packing major ass in his tight cop trousers, I realized Cal and I had a lot of making up to do. As long as he pulled through.

WHERE THE SON DON'T SHINE

$\mathcal{J}$udge $\mathcal{U}$pton had the appearance of a wizened old buzzard who'd seen far too much bad behavior for his own good in his sixty years. His black judge's robes added to the feeling of gloom he conveyed to the people in the courtroom and to the unease he produced in anyone who attracted his attention, his beady eyes appraising them as if they were about to become part of tonight's meal.

He was an ugly old cuss made even more so by the way his lip curled as if the people in his courtroom were some sort of subspecies that he wished to scrape off his shoes before their smell became overpowering. He sniffed as he surveyed his domain. We'd all taken our seats to hear the verdict on Cal's...um...indiscretions.

"The Defendant is young and, I believe, very impressionable. He obviously fell in with a particularly disreputable bunch of older men who took advantage of that naïveté and dragged him through the moral mud into degeneracy of the worst kind. It is to the credit of his father and the young man's own friends that they attempted to rescue him from the mire in which he found himself but was unable to escape because of the conditions in which he was kept by his tormentors. He was drugged, coerced into behavior he would not otherwise have considered."

The snort of derision behind me attracted Upton's displeasure.

"I fail to see the humor in the situation and if you interrupt in such a manner again I will have you removed from the court," Upton said glaring at the perpetrator.

I knew it was either Zach or Clive as they were seated with their lawyers two rows behind me and Cal's support base of Derek, Izzy, Gene and Artie. Although Cal's two cop mates Vinnie and Roy sat apart from us it was not to distance themselves from my son's outrageous conduct but for appearance's sake as they did not want to compromise their position helping him on the sly. It would not do to have Zach and Clive's lawyers see us being too pally with the arresting officers. In private, it was a different matter altogether. The two cops pulled strings wherever they were owed favors.

In fact, I suspected Old Buzzard, still pontificating about the treachery of my three former friends in their debasement of my son, was having his chain yanked as well. I just didn't see how and it was probably better that I didn't.

"I have taken into account that the Defendant is co-operating with police and has turned State's evidence and will be vital in the prosecution of the three individuals, one of whom still has not been apprehended, who are accused of involvement in the drug trade." Upton was droning on in a manner that suggested he was enjoying playing to the gallery, all the power residing in his hands. The tension from behind me was palpable, especially as Zach, Clive and the still missing Phil, had been stitched up by the Drug Squad. As far as I was aware, they'd never had anything at all to do with drugs, except those they'd fed Cal on a regular basis, mainly crystal meth, in order to pimp him out or to take advantage of him themselves. That was sufficiently heinous that most people easily believed the worst of them.

If I'd been in their shoes, I'd be shitting bricks. Cal didn't even have to lie under oath when their trial came up because all he had to do was testify to the trio's force feeding him ice. We'd heard that their defense was that Cal was a willing participant in his own downward spiral and that he was so drug-fucked and aggressive they supplied the prohibited substance to prevent him harming himself. They'd already been asked why they hadn't simply taken him to rehab. We guessed their lawyers were currently working on an answer that was even remotely believable.

"I've taken into account the Defendant's hitherto unblemished character, the remarkable personal reference from his pastor…"

Cal was standing in the dock, his lips curling up in an unmistakable smirk at the mention of his hometown minister. That was something I would have to ask him about.

The judge droned on, his captive audience probably wishing he'd get to the point as much as I did.

"Taking into account the Defendant's previous unblemished record, the superb character references which put paid to the argument that this was anything other than aberrant behavior on his part, and his willingness to testify against those whom he once foolishly considered his friends, I am nevertheless unable to excuse his conduct totally." He paused for breath and shifted his focus to Cal. "I therefore sentence you to six months imprisonment with a non-parole period of ninety days."

There were no gasps or cheering although Cal appeared relieved as he was led away but not before he silently mouthed a 'thank you' to me and the other friends who'd rallied to his defense. As I made my way to the courtroom exit, I was bailed up by a snarling Zach who was purple in the face. "Don't think this is over by any means," he hissed. "Your darling little boy may have got away this time but just wait until we get him on the stand at our trial. Both your reputations will be fucked. And not in a nice way."

He batted away his attorney who was attempting to intervene to get him to shut his mouth.

"Neither of you will be able to show your faces in public. I feel sorry for you, having to lie awake each night imagining the horrors being perpetrated on your innocent little slut by the people in the cells with him. Oh lord, how I would love to see that. Just you remember to watch your back. Phil is still out there and he's angry as hell. You never know what he might do to you or your boy."

Vinnie, who heard the last part of Zach's tirade, intervened. "Is that a threat, sir?" Turning to the lawyers accompanying Zach and Clive, he continued. "I suggest you keep your client on a shorter leash, he's doing himself irreparable damage with every syllable he utters."

Clive glared at me as if it were all my fault but remained mum. I don't think any of us could have predicted how screwed up our lives would become as a result of Cal's cavalier offer of sex to all my friends. But it was on their heads that they'd pushed way beyond the initial 'offer' into territory that included deliberately pimping my son in order to humiliate both of us and drugging him to keep him compliant.

Zach was ushered away screaming until the courtroom door closed on his invective and we could no longer hear him.

As Cal's friends, we were all going to the pub to celebrate because we were relieved it was all over and that we knew he'd be sent to a low-level security prison where he would serve his time, probably the ninety days, and then he'd be back home with me where he belonged.

I'd had only a few brief conversations with him since his arrest after the young cop and I had delivered him to the hospital. Cal was resilient, so after a few days bed rest he was prodded and pricked by not only doctors and nurses who were doing their duty but also by the constable and a group of male orderlies who cheered him up immeasurably by fucking his ass on a regular basis. From the hospital he was taken to the cells until his trial.

The case had been expedited because the prosecution came up with an extraordinarily generous plea bargain in which he would plead guilty to a few very minor charges in exchange for testifying against his captors. It was a no brainer and Cal accepted immediately.

He seemed relieved to be out of his kidnappers' clutches and the second week when I visited him in hospital, he held my hand and with tears in his eyes he said, "I don't know how I can thank you, dad. If it hadn't been for you, I don't know where I'd be today. Probably lying in the gutter somewhere."

I didn't want him dwelling on the past so I put my hand under the blanket and played with his ass, surprised only slightly when my fingers easily slipped inside his spunk-lubed hole. "I think I know of one or two ways you can thank me," I smiled, finger fucking the loads back up inside him before feeding him my greasy hand.

He sucked and licked the spooge greedily. "You know that's always yours any time you want it," he said. "But you don't, that's the trouble."

"These last few weeks have changed me, Cal. The one good thing to come out of all this mess is that it's opened my eyes to how much I need you. How much I want you with me."

Cal appeared sad. "It may already be too late dad. I've changed, too. You may not like me as I am now."

Against my better judgment, I trotted out that old cliché, "You could never do anything to stop me loving you, Cal."

He suddenly got very serious. "Dad, I've got something to tell you...I'm broken goods."

I patted his hand. "It's okay, you can go away to the country for nine months where nobody knows you and then we'll give the baby up for adoption."

Despite himself, he laughed. He went to speak again but I stopped him by putting my finger to his lips.

"You're not broken or perverted or any of the other things that those evil fuckers called you. They drugged you."

"That's the point," he said sadly. "They didn't have to. I would have done it anyway. That's what I discovered about myself."

"I know," I replied.

"You too?"

"They used threats not drugs against me, still I used that to justify my behavior in the beginning when I was beating off at night imagining all sorts of degradation they were committing on you. I was hard for days."

He lost his hangdog look, becoming much more animated than he had been. "Oh, dad, I was so fuckin' hard every time they cuffed me in a public shithouse. And in the club, did you see…?"

"I saw."

"And I don't disgust you?"

I took his hand and placed it over my crotch so he could feel my cock straining for relief.

He smiled wickedly. "What bit turned you on the most?"

That smile was soon wrapped around my cock in his hospital bathroom as I unloaded what felt like gallons of spunk across his tongue.

There had been no further opportunity to consummate our new relationship because he'd been discharged later that afternoon, Vinnie and Roy taking him straight to the cells. Maybe not straight to the cells because I'm sure Cal's bathroom saw a lot of activity. They would probably have to disinfect it after he left.

Vinnie convinced me Cal was safer in the police lock-up until the trial than being out on the streets where he was vulnerable to threats from his three tormentors or even physical violence from Phil who was still on the run. The bastard phoned me late one night to leave drunken menaces that incriminated him and his mates even further. I didn't take them particularly seriously even though his wife, Helen, had instituted divorce proceedings and fled the family home with their baby to live with her sister in the country.

Now that Cal and I had sorted out our differences and chicken shit me, the moral coward, had decided finally to give in to my cock's demands, the minimum three months apart would be hell.

Still, I was grateful for the outcome, after all, Cal could be lying in a gutter somewhere instead of being holed up in a low-security prison where I hoped his ass would be saved the savage use he would get in a maximum security lock-up.

Cal's friends and I were about to adjourn to the pub to celebrate but without the man in question when Vinnie approached to whisper in my ear. "The judge would like to see you in chambers." He must have seen the startled look cross my face because he added quickly, "It's nothing serious. Just to talk about Cal's future."

I relaxed, informing the others in the group that I would join them shortly for a drink, that the judge wanted a few words. As Vinnie led me down the corridor, he eased my mind a little when he said, "Judge Upton is on Cal's side. We pulled a few strings to get him as the trial judge and it worked out pretty well, I think." I nodded agreement. "It'll keep Cal off the streets so we can mop up the rest of the operation, get Clive and Zach to agree to a plea bargain so the whole thing can be kept under wraps which would be in their best interests as well. The wild card is Phil."

When we reached the judge's chambers, Vinnie knocked in what sounded suspiciously like code and Roy opened the door, locking it after we'd entered. Judge Upton was reclining on a leather lounge that dominated one wall of his spacious book-lined office and it was obvious immediately why he needed this degree of security. He was naked, his wizened old cock plugging Cal's mouth as he kneeled on the floor.

Judge Upton greeted me like an old friend even though we'd never met before. "Ah, Buzz, I'll be with you in a moment. Just test driving this slut of yours and I have to say he's a credit to you. His mouth is pure heaven. I hope his ass is as hot as the other place."

Cal was also naked and seemed irritated by the conversation. "Come on, you old fuck, less talking and more action." He stood up, removed the papers and other court items from the top of the judge's ample desk and lay on his back his legs in the air, his ass invitingly moist.

"Ah," the judged sighed. "I do like a lad who embraces his inner slut though in this case I think Cal's is so near the surface as to be his outer slut as well."

I watched as the thin bony judge spat in his hand to grease his semi-limp cock which was obviously his pride and joy and begin to stuff it in Cal's eager butthole. He stopped to look at me. "I assume you have no objections? No, I thought not."

"Punish me, your honor," Cal begged. "Fill my ass with your judge spunk."

"Oh, I will lad, don't you worry."

"I want to feel your hard prick of justice ramming my bad boy butt. Punish me with your prick. Send me to hell and back."

"The pleasure will be all mine."

"You're such an ugly fuckin' old bastard but your cock feels so good inside my shit canal."

I flinched, expecting the judge to baulk at Cal's comments, instead he merely chuckled while his scrawny ass bobbed back and forth as he sank his prick into Cal's guts.

"I bet it excites your dad to see an ugly old fucker like me banging his boy in front of him. Let's take it up a notch, shall we?" Judge Upton leaned forward without missing a stroke and latched his mouth onto Cal's. It was the grossest and most dick hardening thing I'd ever seen. Cal groaned around the judge's invading tongue as his substantial prick, now rock hard, pounded his ass.

Roy and Vinnie also moved uncomfortably, adjusting their crotches as they did so, fascinated by the scene unfolding before them. There was nothing any of us could do until the judge finished which he did with all the finesse of a hog wallowing in mud. He grunted his completion, pulled out, and wiped his prick on a tissue from a box he had close to hand. I wondered if he fucked those who appeared before him on a regular basis. He didn't bother dressing, merely wrapping his judge's cloak around him as he sat at his desk.

Cal wiped his ass with a tissue before he dressed.

"Cal," the judge said. "These two fine policemen told me what your enemies said to your father in the court and although the idea of being thrown in with a lot of the toughs of society sounds like a fantasy come true, it isn't. It's really your worst nightmare."

"Damn," Cal said with a smile although by now I knew him well enough to know he was only half joking.

"But there is a solution, if you wish to take it."

"What choice do I have?"

"I can either send you to a work farm where you'll be comparatively unmolested although I can't guarantee your lawyer won't turn up from time to time to claim payment."

The sneer on Cal's face said all it needed to about that choice.

"On the other hand, I have something that is probably much more to your liking. There is a prison that has managed to keep out of the news although its warden is often accused of being a bleeding heart progressive. However, his new system is certainly getting results although if the press got their hands on it, there would be a national scandal. With your permission, and your father's, I'd like to send you to this facility. The gay inmates are housed in separate wings. Perhaps I should say the inmates who identify as gay. There is little contact between the two wings except…" The judge paused and Cal's interest peaked. "Except once a week, the inmates on both sides who have kept their noses clean are allowed to, shall we say, mingle for a few hours."

"You mean it's a fuckfest?" Cal asked excitedly.

"For those who obey the rules," the judge concurred.

"The system works?" I asked.

"It has so far," the judge replied. "Of course, there are still those who wish to cause problems but missing out on the weekly gangbangs quickly brings them into line. Naturally, the gay men we send to this detention center are… um…a little on what we usually call the slutty side."

"That's Cal," I said.

"Are you both in agreement?"

I looked to Cal and we both nodded at the same time, perhaps he with a little more enthusiasm than me.

"You won't regret it, either of you," the judge said, obviously pleased with his handiwork. Turning to address me, he added, "I've arranged for you to visit the prison during one of these inmate exchanges as I suspect you like to watch. I've arranged it with the warden. He's a good friend of mine. And will be a good friend of yours too, Cal." The judge winked.

It had been arranged for Roy and Vinnie to transport Cal to the prison and I had no doubt their spunk would soon be joining the judge's in Cal's juicy ass. I hugged my son, kissing him passionately and whispered "I love you, Cal," in his ear. He responded in kind. The farewell threatened to become a little mawkish so I shook hands with the judge and made a quick exit intending to head to the pub to join Cal's friends. I must have been preoccupied because I was half-way across the roadway outside the court before I noticed a delivery van bearing down on me, its warning horn surprisingly silent and instead of slowing, it picked up speed.

But for the quick thinking of a passing stranger who yanked me out of the path of the careening vehicle whose side mirror still almost connected with my head, I would have been road kill to be shoveled off the asphalt.

"Fuckwits like that shouldn't be allowed on the roads," my savior said as we watched the vehicle speed off, its number plates strangely blacked out.

"I owe you, big time," I said, still shaking from the near miss. I wouldn't have been so rattled if I hadn't got a near perfect look at the driver as he floored his van toward me. I would swear that it was Phil. He was obviously trying to kill me or at least warn me off.

I was profuse in my thanks even inviting the stranger to the pub for a drink but he seemed the unprepossessing type and begged a prior engagement, even going so far as to refuse a cash reward I offered him. There are still some good guys left in the world.

The other good guys were in the pub lounge eager for news about my meeting with the judge and his offer to incarcerate Cal in a segregated prison for his own protection. I left out the more salacious points of the discussion, afraid that talking about them would only dilute their cock stiffening fantasy potential.

I was exhausted from the weeks of worry about Cal, and now that it was all over and we'd repaired our relationship all I wanted to do was sleep. By the time I got in the front door of the house, my body was about to shut-down although not before my cock got a vigorous work-out from my hand while I replayed all the action in the judge's chambers. I fell asleep a satisfied man.

Life was good again, full of promise, after a few days' rest. I bounced back happier than I had been in ages, managing to clear up a backlog of work that had been awaiting my decisions, too important for even Gene to handle although he'd made notes on each file of the positives and negatives of each. He would make an astute businessman.

I was allowed a visit once a week to see Cal whose initial frustration at having to obey what he considered arbitrary and rather childish rules gave way to unalloyed enthusiasm.

"You know, dad, if it wasn't for the fact I miss you, I think I'd be writing to the judge to ask that I not make parole. I'd be more than happy to spend the entire six months of my sentence in here. Fuck, the guys are hot."

He was putting some of the bulk back on that he'd lost during his enslavement, much of it muscle from working out with the prison weights. We both looked forward to the weekly visits where we discussed our future in general terms. I'd prompted the university to take him back to which they readily agreed after the judge intervened on

Cal's behalf as a character witness. Izzy and Derek promised to keep Cal on the bent and narrow when he moved back home and I offered them a room as well to save them paying for accommodation. They'd proven good friends to Cal, it was the least I could do

It was the third month of Cal's internment before I was permitted to attend the fuckfest, unfortunately not as a participant but as an audience member. I was a guest of the Warden in the guard's box, a sort of Perspex bubble set up as a viewing room and security central above the common area of the prison where the inmates watched TV or played pool or just generally hung about. From there I would be able to see all the action on the floor below and listen in on the conversations. Because the lights would be off in our bubble it would be difficult for those below to watch us, not that they would be particularly interested anyway.

I watched as a few men were confined to their cells.

"They can watch but not touch," the Warden explained. "They can jerk off, we don't have a problem with that, but they can't touch the gay inmates and they usually find that so frustrating they're on their best behavior for a month or so after that. It really does keep the violence down giving them an outlet for their sexual frustration. Far fewer assaults. It doesn't work for everyone, of course, and occasionally we have to move someone out. We've even had a few relationships develop that continue on the outside."

He seemed proud of his achievements.

A cheer went up among the group of around thirty men in the courtyard area below. I saw about six or seven gay men ushered into the wing from another part of the prison. None of them looked in the slightest apprehensive, in fact they were waving and smiling broadly as they entered, some blowing kisses to the men confined behind their locked cells. Cal was in the midst of them and made straight for the biggest and meanest looking bastard in the at-home team. I must have appeared concerned because the Warden said quickly, "That's Jonas. Been as pliable as a puppy since Cal showed up. They have a real thing going. Caused a bit of friction initially. Jonas got jealous and wanted Cal to himself but your son soon put him straight. Now he shares but I think it's still with a certain amount of reluctance. We don't know what's going to happen in a few weeks when we release Cal."

"So soon?"

"His ninety days will be up shortly. The judge never expected we would keep him longer than that even if he proved disruptive. It was mainly to keep him protected from those men who pimped him out, although I hear one of them is still at large."

"It'll be good to have him home," I said.

"We told him you'd be here today so he's been on his extra special best behavior."

Almost as if Cal heard what was said, he looked up at the bubble and waved. Jonas obviously queried his action and Cal explained, a wide smile spreading across the huge prisoner's face as he squeezed Cal's ass and swept him into his muscular tattooed arms. I sensed they were going to put on quite a performance.

A guard blew a whistle and soon the area below was a seething mass of bodies as men in various stages of dress as well as fully naked got down and very dirty. Guards with Tasers patrolled the perimeter of the action while a similar number were perched on the second floor, truncheons and weapons at the ready.

"In all the time I've been here they've never had to use them," the Warden assured me. "But we still have to take precautions."

I saw Jonas tense as Cal shucked his clothes and kneeled on the floor to take another prisoner in his mouth. Jonas had been too slow and lost the opportunity to be the first to fuck Cal's throat that day. He made up for it for shoving three fingers into Cal's butt with the aid of pump packs of lubrication that were scattered around the tables. I thought he was being rougher than absolutely necessary as if attempting to punish Cal, but then again, I knew Cal liked it rough. The rougher the better.

The first guy was fucking Cal's face, choking him so badly I could hear him gag in the security booth. I also heard Jonas, like a carnival barker, shouting, "Come on, guys, feed him. Give him all the cock he wants, drown him in cum. Fuck his pretty boy face until he chokes. Fuck his faggot mouth cunt. You won't see him again for another week."

The Warden suddenly appeared embarrassed and turned to me with abject apology writ large across his features. "I'm so sorry," he muttered. "I should have warned you about the language. It can be quite crude at times. They don't mean anything by it."

"It's fine," I assured him. "Cal likes dirty talk with his sex. In fact, the dirtier and more humiliating, the better."

I knew the only reason Cal was not matching Jonas foul word for foul word was because his mouth was full of hard prison prick.

Looking around the orgiastic excess that was unfolding downstairs, I noticed each gay man had a pack of admirers working him over, some of the men grabbing quick oral before moving on to the next boy to test who had the technique he liked best. A few men even stood apart smoking, watching the action, waiting their turn to join in. There was an unhurried air to the activity, as if they knew they had plenty of time in which to indulge their appetites, no need for furtive fucking, going at it like a steam hammer. Although there was room for that if you wanted it.

These men looked as if they wanted gourmet sex not a quickie and the gay boys were supplying it in spades. There were a couple of them I wouldn't mind sticking on the end of my cock for a bit of fun myself.

Jonas had finished greasing up Cal's fuck hole because he was now spruiking the joys of fucking him while holding his ass cheeks apart. My son was fairly oblivious to the whole exercise as he was concentrating on yet another prison cock ramming his mouth. One of the guys on the fringe dropped his cigarette and stubbed it out with his foot. He was unbuckling his belt and unzipping his fly as he strode toward Cal's ass and without so much as an introduction, spat in his hand, jerked his cock and sank between the lubricated cheeks, bellowing with pleasure.

Jonas wandered off to test the oral skills of one or two of the other gay boys but always kept an eye on Cal whether for safety reasons or because of jealousy I was not quite sure. Either way, my little boy was a glutton for cock and seemed to be enjoying himself immensely. I must admit, though, after about twenty minutes there was a sameness to the activity and there was not much to keep a voyeur satisfied, especially as we were too distant to feel part of the action. We might as well have been watching it on a screen.

A couple of guys had unloaded in Cal's ass because I could see the glisten of spunk dribbling from his battered hole each time one of the prisoners pulled out.

"We have to hose the place down when it's all over. Stinks of cum and lubrication for days," the Warden said. "It's a bit on the boring side for the next few hours until the guard gives them the half-hour whistle and then things get a bit frantic. Would you care to join me in my office? Or stay if you would prefer."

"No, I'll join you, thanks for the offer."

As we were buzzed through the security gate, the Warden said, "It's well worth returning for the last half hour, the feeling of sex and testosterone in the air is so palpable the guards get into it shouting encouragement, especially those on the floor downstairs. If any of the gay boys wants to take on one or two of the guards because they haven't had enough, well, we tend to turn a blind eye to such activity. There's no shortage of volunteers for the job that way."

"You have it all worked out," I laughed.

We enjoyed a pleasant hour or so, he eventually admitting he'd indulged in sampling Cal's ass, pushed into the unprofessional behavior by the raves of some of his guards. He'd found it to his liking and would have liked even more to continue the affair, reluctant to let Cal escape at the end of the ninety days.

"Nothing much I can do about it," he sighed. "You have friends in high places. It's all mapped out. Even had Cal murdered someone while in my prison he would have been released at the end of the ninety days."

I was impressed because I had no idea who these friends in high places were. Cal had never mentioned them and I hardly thought the description applied to the old buzzard Upton. I made a mental note to question Vinnie and Roy on the subject; they seemed to know more about what was going on than anyone else.

We made our way back to the booth in time for the half-hour whistle. The men looked much the worse for the experience, the gay bottoms in particular covered in sweat and snail trails of dried as well as fresh spunk across their face and bodies, their asses leaking spooge like ripe runny camembert. A few stalwarts were still plugging the boys while most sat about smoking or chatting until the time was up. Billy was on all fours with Jonas riding his butt like a rodeo cowboy screaming his appreciation. "This is the most rancid asshole I've ever fucked. It so full of jail spunk he'll be shittin' our baby batter for days. His sweet little bud of fuckin' pleasure is so stretched he's like a back-alley whore. Fuckin' slut boy, tell me how bad you want it."

"Fuck me, sir. Make me your sex slave. I'll do anything you want, sir, 'cause I need your cock so bad. Fuck my slut ass in front of my dad, humiliate me, sir. Dominate me. Show me what a whore I am."

They kept it up for another ten minutes the language getting more and more foul as Jonas came up with ways to totally control Cal. I must admit I was as hard as the Warden seemed to be, for his breath was coming in short bursts. The guard blew his whistle again and Jonas yelled his orgasm pumping his seed into Cal's butthole.

"I think you'll enjoy this," the Warden warned, and from the glazed look in his eyes I could see that he would. "This was all Cal's idea after he saw that movie, *The Human Centipede*."

I was stunned that the Warden allowed that sort of movie in his prison. But then, what did I know?

"Cal persuaded the other gay boys to be in it and they seemed very keen. One or two didn't much like the idea but this group were all for it."

The boys moved to the center of the floor and got down on all fours one directly behind the other shuffling until they formed a rough circle, facing the ass of the boy in front. Then they parted his butt with their hands in order to sink their lips around his leaking spunk hole, sucking and licking the cum from the freshly fucked ass. It was awkward with so few men in the circle but they managed to siphon out huge quantities of slime until their faces shone with the elixir of life. Finally, the guard blew his whistle and the boys broke, the inmates applauding their efforts. It would be a week before they repeated the exercise.

I saw Cal for five minutes with the Warden's permission, tasting a dozen men's sperm as he kissed me passionately his body slimy with men's desire.

"I was so proud of you, son. You did well," I said.

"It was fun having you watch, just a pity you couldn't join in." Cal looked accusingly at the Warden, and then threw his hands up in mock defeat. "I know, I know, it's against prison regulations."

The Warden left us to continue our conversation in private. Cal got very serious. "Dad, are you sure you know what you're getting into by having me back home? I'm damaged goods. I like my life now. The guys are not kidding when they call me a slut and a whore. I don't want to make life difficult for you."

"Nothing you do will upset me," I said.

"I'm more concerned about what I did in the past," he said. I could see he meant it.

"I'm pretty sure I know most of it, if not all."

"I'll only end up disgusting you," he admitted sadly.

"Is this your way of telling me you've changed your mind about me?" I dreaded his answer.

"God, no. Never think that. You're my life, dad."

"Then it's settled. Your friends are looking forward to having you back. They're organizing a party for your return."

"I look forward to it, dad. Look, I gotta go. You'll come and see me next week?"

"Wouldn't miss it," I said cheerfully. "And a week after that I'll be at the gate to drive you home."

On the drive back to the city I tried to figure out a way to show Cal that nothing he could do or had done would disappoint me or disgust me. I racked my brain for an idea but came up blank. I would have to get input from the others, this was too important to screw up. It was only after I stopped worrying about it, that the most obvious solution jumped straight into my head. I didn't want to lose the momentum so I dialed Vinnie on my hands free and set the surprise in motion.

I must have been concentrating too hard on the call because a van suddenly shot out of a side entrance ramp in front of me and I had to brake hard to avoid a collision, my car sliding onto the edge of the expressway as the car behind narrowly missed me. I cursed my lack of attention although I could have sworn when I looked at the ramp the car was stationary in a lay-by. It wasn't until I compared the van make and color with the one that had almost flattened me outside the court that I began to worry it may have been deliberate.

Too late to catch up with the vehicle in question, I realized its number plates would have been disguised with mud or some other impediment anyway. I'd better let Vinnie and Roy know my suspicions although I wondered whether I was paranoid. I didn't wonder for long.

As I pulled into the driveway of my home, I saw the front door was ajar. Admittedly, Derek and Izzy had a key as they'd be moving their gear in shortly but it was unlike them to leave the premises vulnerable if they weren't around and I couldn't see any indication they were about.

I was wary as I pushed open the door, my finger on speed dial on my phone, ready to scream bloody murder if anyone jumped out from a dark corner. No one did but I hit dial anyway.

"I'm on it already," Vinnie said irritably down the phone, meaning the favor I had asked of him less than twenty minutes ago.

"I think you need to get over here asap."

"What's up?"

"And call an ambulance."

His voice changed to serious. "Are you okay, Buzz?"

"I feel like I'm gonna throw up the entire contents of my stomach any minute."

"Where are you?"

"I'm at home," I said, the shakes beginning to rattle my nerves as well as my bones. "The front door was open when I got back. I thought it might be Izzy or Derek because they've got a key. But…"

The rest of the sentence was lost as I threw up my guts on the living room carpet, fortunately missing Izzy's mutilated body that lay sprawled across the divan now crimson from his blood. A warning was written large on the living room wall in what appeared to be that same blood.

CAL IS NEXT!

THE SON SHINES OUT OF HIS ASS

$\mathcal{R}$oy and $\mathcal{V}$innie, the Laurel and Hardy of crime detection, arrived the same time as the ambulance. I'd upchucked on the carpet which would qualify as contaminating a crime scene – big time! – while I was speaking to the two cops who told me to get out of the house and wait: they'd do the rest.

I hated to leave Izzy without at least testing for a pulse but then realized that Roy's advice was timely. Even if he did have a pulse, what could I do about it? The clincher was that the killer might still be in the house because, so far, I had not ventured any farther than the living room. I shuddered as I glanced at the warning written in blood on the wall and after a rather feeble, "Hang in there, Izzy, help is on the way" as, I hoped, some sort of encouragement if he were still alive, I went outside to wait on the front lawn.

My life was fucked in so many ways. Once Izzy was taken care of and after Cal was released from prison I would have to take stock. It was time for a massive reappraisal of where I was headed as the only choices at the moment seemed like jail or the madhouse. Neither held much appeal even had I managed to wangle a deal like Cal did. Also, I'm not young and attractive like he is. I smiled. A slut, yes, but…Like father, like son.

I tensed as I heard the siren off in the distance, getting closer. If the killer was still inside he'd make a dash for it and the only thing standing between him and freedom was me. Foolishly, I was sitting on the grass with my back to the house in a vain attempt to shut the image of a blood-spattered Izzy from my mind. I'd left the front door open as instructed.

The sound of steps on the front porch set my heart racing into overdrive. How could I have been so stupid as to turn my back on danger? My skin crawled at the vulnerability of my position on the grass. My muscles clenched in preparation for springing to my feet to confront whoever it was I could hear advancing slowly in my direction. I had no weapon, nothing with which to defend myself but all I had to do was keep the bastard in the yard until the police or the paramedics arrived. Even if they couldn't hold him, at least they'd be able to identify him in court.

I sprang to my feet and turned, still crouching to make myself a smaller target. I cried out in horror as the gory creature headed toward me, its arms outstretched pleading, the remaining contents of my stomach threatening to explode out of me. I ran toward the house just in time to catch Izzy as he fell forward, his body slippery and difficult to hold because of the blood which spattered my clothes and my body. We were in that bloody embrace as the ambulance and the cops screamed to a halt in the street.

All I remember is gentle hands prizing Izzy out of my grip and concerned paramedics examining me for injury, the crackle of the police radio as Roy called for back-up and, finally, the all-clear as Roy and Vinnie searched the house for the attacker. We all assumed it was Phil, who was still at large.

"You won't want to be spending the night here," Vinnie said.

"Apart from the fact it's a crime scene?" I said sarcastically.

He didn't take offense.

"You got somewhere to stay?"

"I can doss down at the office. It's always set up for emergencies and it'll do for a week or so."

"I'll drive you over myself, make sure you get there okay. Roy will drive your car over later, check to see if he's followed."

I laughed. "Phil knows where I work, Vinnie. Thanks, but I'll drive myself. "

"Don't worry, mate. We'll get him."

I wasn't sure if Vinnie was attempting to assure me or himself. Either way, I don't think he had much success as he looked decidedly dispirited.

The guys did allow me back into the house, via the back door, to gather clothes, my laptop, and any other necessaries

I'd need for my stay at the office. It would be a while before I could return to the house, assuming that I wanted to. Cal's homecoming was going to be a real downbeat affair.

I was loading my car when I realized that in my daze I'd forgotten…I turned to Roy who was directing cops to canvass the area for any witnesses who saw a visitor or visitors to my house.

"Derek…"

"All taken care of, mate. I had a car pick him up and take him straight to the hospital."

"Thanks." My voice was choked with relief, gratitude and sheer fatigue.

"You okay to drive yourself?"

"Yeah. I'll take it easy."

"We'll be over in a couple of hours once we clear up this mess and drop in on Izzy to see if he can give us an ID on his attacker. Get yourself some snooze time, clear your head."

"Thanks, Roy."

I don't remember much of the journey because my head was buzzing with questions, but I was grateful I wasn't pulled over for erratic driving. It would have been difficult to explain the remnants of blood on my arms and face which didn't rub off with the cat wash the cops allowed me. Plus I had my blood spattered clothes in a plastic bag on the back seat. That would take some explaining although a quick call to Roy or Vinnie would settle the matter. The local cops, however, weren't the brightest tuna in the can, noted more for their brutality than their intelligence.

I was never so glad to reach the factory, parking the car out of sight in the loading dock before pulling down the shutters. Suddenly, I was afraid. It was dark inside with enough corners and alcoves that anyone could lie in wait. I didn't think for a minute Phil would be as stupid as to try it with me but the mind plays funny tricks when you're feeling vulnerable.

I'd made enough noise to alert the entire neighborhood, had there been one, when I first arrived, but the area was deserted after hours. A cry for help would go unanswered in this lonely industrial oasis of trucking containers, small businesses, and large machinery yards, as well as a fair number of empty offices, victims of the economic downturn.

It was no use attempting to make my presence less obvious as anyone hiding in the building would have heard me already, so I switched on the lights and generally did everything apart from whistling to keep my spirits up. It proved an unnecessary precaution as Phil was as elusive as the bogeyman although the idea of a visit from either made me lock the door to my makeshift bedroom as well as arm myself with a solid iron bar within reach of the bed.

Hammering on the shutter door woke me. I stumbled in the dark forgetting where I was and it wasn't until I stubbed my toes that I remembered my predicament. I flicked the light switch, reaching for my mobile phone which was vibrating on the small chest of drawers beside the bed. It was Roy to inform me it was him banging on the door, so I dressed hurriedly to let he and Vinnie into the factory.

They came bearing gifts: strong coffee, beer, and takeaway Thai. My small boardroom proved an ideal spot for our aromatic meal and mini-conference.

"Whoever it was knew what he was doing," Roy said between mouthfuls of Chicken Pad Thai. "Izzy will be fine. His injuries are bad but not life threatening. The doctor thinks it was to produce as much blood as possible to scare you and to write the message on the wall. Yeah, it's Izzy's blood."

The delicious meal was clearing my head and filling my belly so I could think again. "So he didn't identify Phil?"

"Afraid not. The attacker got him from behind," Vinnie added. "Knocked him out cold. Cut him while he was unconscious."

"May have been an afterthought when he discovered it wasn't you," Roy suggested.

"Maybe."

Roy addressed my concerns. "Izzy will recover. Derek is staying at the hospital tonight and we've placed a guard on the room just in case. We don't think Phil or whoever is likely to try again. We don't think he tried to kill him."

"That's a relief at any rate." I was glad there was some good news.

There wasn't anything much I could add to the information I'd given the cops earlier but we went over it once again. They grilled me especially about the van that had attempted to run me over and also run me off the road. I gave them a hazy description because it was long gone on both occasions before it had registered as more than a coincidence.

"If Phil had been driving the van when he tried to run you off the highway would he have had time to get to your house before you…?" Vinnie left the remainder unsaid.

"He would have had to drive like the clappers but he might have just managed. Anyway, there's nothing to say Phil doesn't have an accomplice or that it wasn't Clive or Zach. They are out on bail." I was bitter that the judge had released them to torment Cal.

"If they come within cooee of Cal when he's released the judge will lock them up and throw away the key," Vinnie assured me.

I wasn't convinced.

"Speaking of Cal…" Roy was eager to discuss my boy's homecoming.

We were all keen to make it the best possible even though his time incarcerated was anything but a chore as he was getting ganghanged on a regular basis from the prisoners.

"I think he's found his niche in life," I sighed.

Roy mistook my sigh for sadness. "He'll grow out of it. Anyway. Being a slut is not all that terrible."

Vinnie shot him a dirty look that made me laugh. "Shit, I don't care if he's a slut. That's great in my book. He's just like his old man but better at it. But he thinks he's not good enough for me anymore, that it's too much to ask of me because he loves wallowing in degradation. I told him it turns me on but he won't listen. I have to prove it to him."

"And we were glad to help," Vinnie said, clapping me on the shoulder in obvious support.

"I just hope his present does the trick."

The rest of the evening was spent on the logistics of Cal's release and ride back to the city. I was originally going to ferry him home myself but under the circumstances I had to agree with Roy it was preferable he get a ride in a marked police car to prevent a repeat of the van incident. Besides, I had things to plan now that the party had to be moved to the factory.

The following day I went to visit Izzy in hospital. His head was bandaged where he'd been hit from behind, and he looked pale and sickly, stitches in the slashes on his arms and face. He was admiring himself in a hand mirror as I entered his room after being checked off the list by the cop outside.

"If these wounds scar I think it will give me a very macho appearance, don't you?" he asked Derek as I entered.

"No one will dare tangle with you ever again," I said, pleased to see him so chirpy after his ordeal.

His eyes were sunken with traces of purple surrounding them as if the beginning of black eyes but he managed a welcoming smile when I handed him my gifts of flowers and chocolates.

"I wasn't sure if…"

"He loves chocolate," Derek said, attempting to confiscate them from him as he tore off the cellophane. "It'll more likely to be the death of him than anything else."

During my visit I spent most of the time apologizing for what happened until they'd both had enough, ordering me to stop. They were pleased, however, when I told them that because of the state of the house and because I didn't think it was advisable for them to be living in close proximity to either Cal or me for the present, I'd arranged a rental on a small apartment near the university which would suit them fine for Izzy's recovery. I'd taken care of the deposit and the rent.

"You're not to worry about anything," I said, interrupting the profusion of thanks. "If you need anything at all don't hesitate to ring. If I'm not there, I've instructed Gene to give you what you need. And don't worry about your medical bills. That's taken care of as well."

I made a quick exit after that as I didn't want Izzy or Derek to feel particularly beholden to me. It was because of Cal and I that Izzy was in his current situation so I considered my recompense was fair.

It was business as usual over the next two weeks although I was wary enough that I was extra cautious crossing the street and when out driving. On my trip out to see Cal I was so tense behind the wheel I thought something would snap – even if it was just my nerves. Of course, Cal had heard about the assault on Izzy and the message scrawled in blood although it didn't seem to faze him. Concerns for his safety in the prison resulted in the warden isolating Cal for his own protection to the extent that there was talk about canceling his weekly group activity. He kicked up such a fuss that he was reinstated although the participants were culled to manageable numbers and to those prisoners the authorities trusted.

It was Cal's farewell and he wanted to show his mates a good time. In the end, he was the good time had by all. Later, he received another round of farewell spunk from the warden and a few of the guards. If Phil's influence was widespread it didn't seem to have infiltrated the prison.

Cal was disappointed that I wasn't going to pick him up on his release but I put the smile back on his face with the information Roy and Vinnie were to be his police escort and that they'd probably insist on payment on the way back.

Cal was released on the Thursday so I gave the staff an extra two days off so he and I could spend time together without interruption and he could also accommodate a few days of solid buggering with his mates. I'd set up a sling in a little-used part of the factory, away from prying eyes where Cal could take his preferred partners for a bit of fun although it was large enough in area to fit a good baker's dozen as well as the boy himself.

Izzy had insisted on helping out even though he was still shaky on his feet and in a bit of pain although the drugs helped. His stitches were out but the skin was tight where he's been cut. He spent his time painting a large WELCOME HOME CAL banner which we hung across the loading dock where Roy and Vinnie would drop him off.

They'd brought over my gift to Cal, the one that I hoped would prove my love for him and also prove beyond all doubt that I accepted the behavior he thought was too degenerate to be worthy of love. How wrong he was. My love for my little boy had grown with every single day he was away from me. I was bursting with pride as well as lust for him, hoping I'd get some quality time alone before the end of the weekend. We had a lot to discuss.

Roy's signal was a brief burst of the siren on approach so we all took up our positions in the semi darkness. The police car pulled into the loading bay and Roy quickly pulled down the shutter plunging the area into total blackout.

I flicked the switch and the overhead lights illuminated the scene as his friends popped out of their hiding place yelling "Surprise" to Cal's astonishment. I noticed him thumb moisture from the corner of his eye as he was glad handed from one friend to another, Izzy waiting at the end of the line in his wheelchair. Cal hugged him affectionately, kissing him on the forehead.

When all the gushing and well-wishing were tapering off I signaled to the DJ and dance music burst over the PA system. The food, enough to feed an army, was set up on trestle tables and the bar in one corner was already busy.

"Thanks, dad," Cal grinned, wrapping his arms around me. The electric charge went straight to my cock. He must have felt it as well because he palmed the bulge in my trousers, murmuring, "I missed you, too."

"We'll take care of that later," I said encircling him tight enough I never wanted to let him go.

"I'm spoiled goods, dad. You know that," he said seriously. "I'm no good."

"Listen, Cal, I love you. Not just as your dad. That goes without saying. But I also love you like a lover. I love what you are."

"I'll only disappoint you, dad."

"You'll only disappoint me if you keep up this rubbish about being damaged goods. Give it a rest, Cal. We can discuss it later after all your friends have had a chance to welcome you back."

"Okay. Then we talk. I don't think you realize just how degraded I like it now."

"Oh, I think I do," I said. "To prove it, I got you a little present for your homecoming."

In his excitement he became a child again, begging me to give it to him.

"You wait right here and I'll bring it down to you."

"Hurry, dad. I love surprises."

I went up to my office, my heart in my mouth in case my gift didn't work in the way I wanted it to. It would show him I didn't judge his behavior, in fact, I reveled in it, wanted to be part of it. I was so nervous as I went back to the party with his surprise that I almost wet myself. Cal had his back to me but as the other partygoers registered what I was holding, a hush, pregnant with expectation, fell over the crowd.

He turned slowly, and then his face lit up. I'd chosen well.

"Oh my God," he shouted. He fell to his knees and whistled. "Here Luci, here boy."

I let the lead go as the dog wagged its tail in excitement at seeing Cal again and bounded across the factory floor flinging itself at Cal, standing on its hind legs to lick his face, its excitement obvious to everyone at the party.

Later, when things settled, Cal fed and watered Lucifer before sheepishly making his way over to where I'd been watching him.

"Thanks, dad. I owe you."

"You don't owe me anything," I said.

"You understand then?"

"Of course, I do."

"You don't mind."

"I told you, my little boy makes me hot."

"Just like my dad makes me hot."

He pulled my head down to kiss him and as I pushed my tongue into his mouth I tasted the pungent remnants of spunk.

"Sweet," I sighed.

The party unfolded pretty much as I expected: dancing, boozing, eating, and a prodigious amount of fucking and sucking in and around the sling. Just about everyone had a turn, including Izzy, and a few even asked me for permission. That made a change and I gave it freely. I watched from a darkened corner as some of the partygoers spat out abuse as they fucked Cal's ass or his face. Those were the ones who turned me on the most and obviously delighted Cal as well. Some were furtive and silent, others seemed almost grateful for a chance at the fabled asshole that was so popular it overflowed with spunk by the end of the night.

Roy and Vinnie were among the best performers and I could see Cal had a soft spot for them as well as for Gene and Artie and Izzy and Derek.

As Artie rammed his gaping fuck hole, I heard Cal say to Gene, "You guys are so lucky to have each other. I'd love to have a relationship like yours."

Gene laughed. "You already do, mate. You and your dad are the closest relationship I've ever seen. He loves you, Cal."

"Look at me. I'm not much of a catch. My first night out of jail and I'm flat on my back while all his mates fuck me. What sort of a boyfriend does that make me?"

"An ideal boyfriend in your dad's eyes."

Cal's newly minted morality worried me. I thought presenting him with Lucifer would reveal the depth of my feeling for him but it obviously wasn't enough. It wasn't the only thing that worried me that night. I thought Cal appeared bored at times even while his ass was being buggered hard. I made sure he knew I was watching but that didn't seem to have the same frisson as before either. There was something missing. The awful truth of the matter was: I felt the same way.

In the early hours of the morning when everyone's energy was flagging and a number of people had gone home because they were working the next day and others lay asleep on makeshift beds around the factory floor, I helped Cal out of the sling where he had lain and endured for the best part of two hours.

"Send them home, dad."

"I thought you'd want to spend the next three days on your back."

"I did. But I'd rather spend my time with you."

After the party remnants had departed Cal kissed me, his spunk breath overpowering as I ran my hands across his beautiful butt to finger his battered slime hole. Three fingers slipped easily inside stirring the spunk custard that was waiting to ooze out of him. I found his prostate in all that spooge and ran my finger across the little nodule until he shuddered. I kept at it until he almost lost control, panting his desire. At last, I got the result I was after.

"Fuck me, dad."

I was eager to comply. Cal was naked and I had my trousers and underwear off in record time, pushing him roughly against the factory wall.

"Spread your legs, cunt, and bend forward."

"Yes, sir," he croaked.

"I'm gonna make you come, fucker. You're gonna be my own personal cum dump. I'm gonna unload in your sweet hole."

"Yes, sir. Please fuck me," he pleaded.

Cal was more animated now than he had been all night.

I coated my cock with the juice leaking from his butt hole, then aimed and pressed into him roughly.

"Shit, yeah. Fuck me hard," he demanded. "Make it hurt."

As I banged my prick into his guts I felt for his nipples, pinching them severely, digging my thumb nail into the sensitive buds. He groaned, hissing every now and then when the pain shot to his brain. His insatiable ass thrust back to meet my strokes, devouring my cock with an appetite that would never be sated. This was the Cal I loved.

"This is how I love you best, Cal. The insatiable cock slut, the fuck whore, the cum dump for any man who has the guts to shove his prick into that sweet fuck hole. I want to watch you debase yourself until you find the real Cal."

"Fuck me, daddy. Fuck me with the cock that made me when you buried it in mum's cunt. Treat me like a whore daddy. Breed me. Shoot your hot spunk inside me. Fill my ass with all my little brothers."

We were in a world of our own. The party crowd had taken their turn with Cal, now it was my turn, and I would make it count. His ass was mine, his body was mine, his life was mine.

"I made you, Cal. You belong to me. You'll be my fuck toy forever. Your ass has my name stamped on it. I own you, boy, don't ever forget it."

I squeezed his balls so hard he cried out in genuine pain, the sound of it setting my balls aflame so I spewed my junk right up inside his asshole as he ground his butt against me to drain every last drop out of me.

"You didn't come," I said as I felt his cock.

"No, dad. I saved that for you. All those months in jail they took care of my ass but no one took care of my cock. So, old man, it's your turn. Spread 'em."

I took up a position similar to his, my breath still ragged in my lungs. He dribbled spunk into his hand from his ass and used it to lubricate my hole and his own cock. He was no more gentle than I was and I thought he'd rip me apart as he rammed into me. I flinched as he had no regard for the pain he was inflicting until I managed to relax and the pleasure took over.

"You like my cock in your ass, daddy? Your little boy's hard prick inside your shit hole? Gonna fill you with son spunk, breed your incestuous ass just like you bred mine. You're fuckin' scum, daddy, just like me. We fit together so perfect. Don't you agree?"

"Yes, Cal," I whimpered. "We were made for each other. Father and son. Fuckers against morality with nothing to lose."

"You said it, dad. You know something? I've been so bored all night. All those cocks. Yeah, they were fun, but nothing like yours. You know how to play me, dad."

"Just like you know how to play me, son. I saw how bored you were. And I was bored, too. I wanted you to break out, be yourself. I never want you to hold back, Cal."

Cal was panting now. He broke the game in genuine surprise. "You serious, Buzz?"

"Deadly."

"You'll still love me, no matter what?"

"No matter what."

"No matter how black my fantasies are?"

"They'll just match mine."

"Oh, dad. Take me to hell with you."

He howled like a dog as he unloaded inside me, splashing my bowels with his warm spooge. We collapsed on the floor together, lying like that for heaven knows how long only waking when Lucifer began to lick our sweaty bodies, his tongue slobbering on our skin.

When he started on our faces we were in serious danger of drowning. That did it. We roused ourselves and crawled up to the bedroom. Lucifer had already become accustomed to sleeping on the floor at the foot of my bed so he naturally took up that spot as Cal and I clambered under the sheets, far too tired to indulge our appetites further.

Roy was one of the last to leave earlier, telling me he'd escort the stragglers off the premises and would lock up before he left. I had to trust him because I was too fucked to check.

The next few days passed uneventfully. Roy and Vinnie came over on the weekend to report on the lack of progress over Izzy's assault. They were honest enough to say it was unlikely they'd ever catch the culprit unless he or she confessed. It didn't make it any less irritating to hear put honestly what I'd already suspected. They warned Cal about venturing out alone especially as Zach, Clive and Phil were just itching to get their hands on him for revenge. They thought he was quite safe in the factory but if he wanted to venture out they suggested that he take Artie as a bodyguard.

Cal and I talked and talked until we were sick of our own voices. He was as indecisive as a two-headed cow about our relationship. One moment he was clinging to me as if I were his inseparable twin while at other times he bemoaned his degeneracy and the fact he doubted I could love anyone as morally stained as he was. Those were his own words and I eventually had to ban him from discussing himself in terms of sin, morality or stains on his character. Soiled or broken were also verboten.

Although his friends dropped by for chats and sometimes sex he was going stir crazy to the extent he sometimes wished he was back in prison.

"I had more fun than this when I was in jail," he said.

He took to wandering around the factory floor in the tightest shorts he could find, his ass cheeks hanging out, flirting with the workers. He became so disruptive Artie came to me pleading.

"Buzz, the guys aren't pulling their weight when Cal is on the floor. Do something about it. Please."

"You're the foreman, Artie. Can't you do something?"

"Yeah, right. Ban the boss's son. I'd like to keep my job, if it's all the same to you."

Gene was listening to the conversation. "What do the men think about Cal? Are they fag haters?"

"A couple of the guys muttered about the boss's fag son but I soon put them right."

Gene persevered. "What about the others?"

Artie went red in the face. "Look, I'd rather not say."

I saw where Gene's questioning was headed.

"They'd fuck him if the slut wasn't the boss's son?" I smiled as I said it to show I wasn't upset.

"Well, a blow job at least. The word has got around about his skill in that department."

"Right, in that case, Artie, could you drop a gentle hint or two on the floor that the boss is oblivious to the fact his son is a fag slut but as long as it doesn't interfere with work and it's discreet, you have no objections to them using him as a cum dump on a regular basis."

"You sure, Buzz?"

"Positive. In fact, tell them you've tried him yourself and can recommend him."

Artie muttered as he turned to leave. "I don't know about this."

"And Artie. Don't tell Cal that I said it was okay. Let him think it's a secret between him and the men."

He shook his head as if he thought I was out of my mind. "You're the boss."

After he left I turned to Gene. "Did I do the right thing?"

"Definitely. Cal's like a caged animal. He needs an outlet for all that energy. I suggest you put some second-hand bedding down in that corner where you hung the sling for the party. An old mattress or something. Don't be obvious. Half hide it somewhere the guys are sure to find it. They'll do the rest. What's even better, there's a walkway above it. You can watch the action from there. If the mood strikes you."

"Oh, it will. It definitely will."

I left Gene with instructions to put the bedding in place. I would have done it myself except I had to take a phone call from Irene, my ex-wife.

"Where the hell is Cal?" she screamed down the phone.

"Fine, thank you, Irene. And you?"

The sarcasm totally escaped her and she just screamed the same question, this time louder.

"If you mean at this precise moment, I don't know. If you mean where he is today, then I can tell you he's working in the factory."

It doesn't hurt to stretch the truth a little with Irene.

"I haven't heard from him in three months. What the fuck is going on?"

It was unlike Irene to swear. It was serious.

"He went away to do some serious thinking about his future, Rene." I always abbreviated her name when I was trying to get her onside. "It was his time alone in the desert." I hoped the biblical reference would appeal to her fundamentalist nature. "I told him to drop you a line or give you a call at least once a month. Didn't he do that?"

"No, he did not, as well you know."

"No, I didn't know that, Rene. All I know is he didn't keep in touch with me so I had to assume he was okay. He came back last Thursday."

"And why aren't you answering your phone at home?"

I took a deep breath. "I haven't been there for a couple of weeks. The house was broken into while I was at work and the vandals did a lot of damage. They shit on the carpets and the furniture and scrawled obscenities on the walls."

"I'm not surprised, the lifestyle you're living. The people you must mix with. I hope you keep them well clear of Cal. He's very impressionable, you know."

If you only knew the half of it.

"Anyway, I'm living at the office for a while and Cal is staying here with me. He's earning his keep by working in the factory."

"Good. Look, Buzz, I don't mind telling you that bad news and gossip travels fast. We've heard things over here that are so unbelievable they would make your hair stand on end. At church the other day, Miss Fitton swore she has a friend who heard that Cal was in prison."

"I suppose she heard it from a friend of a friend of her aunt's or something like that? Did she happen to say why Cal was in jail?"

"Something to do with an auction, she said."

"I'm not sure how they do auctions in your part of the world but over here they are well-run and regulated and I can assure you that no one goes to jail for attending an auction. You can tell your Miss Fitton she's talking bullshit."

"I want to speak to him, Buzz."

"I'll get him to call you when his shift finishes."

"Now!"

I tried everything but she remained adamant. In the end I called Cal over the tannoy because she didn't trust me not to coach him if I went personally to find him on the factory floor. She thought this way she could curtail any collusion. She reckoned without my ability to scrawl bullet points on a sheet of paper as Cal walked through the office door. I cautioned him to be quiet as I handed it to him. He read quickly and then nodded his head.

"Here he is, Rene. I'll put him on."

Cal was a quick study, verifying basically what I had told her, embellishing just enough to make it sound truthful. She wasn't placated but was reassured, according to Cal. He had to do copious *mea culpas* to obtain forgiveness but he stressed how important the alone time was to his development. She bought it. Not, however before she informed him that the pastor at the nearest church of the denomination she followed would drop in to see him some time the following week. Just to check on his welfare.

Shit!

I wondered whether the local preacher was where Miss Fitton had gleaned her information. The story of Cal's arrest and the raid on the biker club had made the papers, fortunately not on the front page as the details were much too scandalous for the general populace. Still it had appeared buried about page eight and anyone with a computer and a modicum of literacy would be able to search for it merely by entering Cal's birth name. If my memory served me well, there was a photograph of Cal being bundled into court. I remember the picture as blurred and indistinct but I would lay odds that Irene would recognize her own son.

I called an emergency meeting of Gene and Artie plus Roy and Vinnie to hammer out some sort of plan. Cal, of course, was involved but seemed eager to get away even though it was his future at stake. His fidgeting was such a distraction that I told him he was excused, that I'd relay the details to him later. He rushed from the room in such a hurry I knew where he was headed. I caught Gene's eye and he as good as confirmed he was thinking the same thing I was.

Ten minutes later, I left the meeting, ostensibly to relieve my bladder but instead I headed for the walkway above the area set aside for Cal's liaisons, annoyed that he favored them above discussions about his own safety. There was a time and a place for cock and Cal would have to learn that.

Sure enough, he was kneeling on the filthy old mattress while one of the workmen stuffed his mouth with cock. Another two were standing stroking their pricks, waiting their turn. It was hot seeing Cal taking on all comers regardless of body type and looks. He was a real cock slut and it made me hard just thinking about it. I could have remained and taken myself in hand, but the meeting took precedence.

On my return, Gene outlined his plan to ensure the preacher came to the office rather than wandering around the factory floor with the distinct possibility he would run across Cal indulging his voracious sexual appetite. If we could control the meeting we might get away with it. We would have to tell Cal to keep a pair of loose fitting overalls near to hand to throw over his revealing shorts in case of the unscheduled visit.

Roy mentioned something about witness protection but that was several steps too far to contemplate for even a moment. Vinnie suggested a check on the preacher to see if he had any secrets of his own but the Reverend Nigel Calhoun came up cleaner than the proverbial whistle. Disappointing.

If Cal was going stir crazy I was feeling as if the walls were closing in on me. I wondered how long we could keep up the pretense and whether Cal was right, we should call a halt to our relationship and go our separate ways. There were two things against it: I loved him, and I knew without someone to keep an eye out for him he would self-destruct.

Artie was brought up to speed on the events. His job was to keep Cal under surveillance and ensure the preacher did not get an opportunity to wander around unaccompanied. Cal sat still long enough to receive instruction on his part in the deception and I already knew he was a good enough actor that he might convince an otherworldly preacher man. We had to pray that Calhoun was as naïve as the dogma he espoused.

Over the next few days we planned for every contingency we could anticipate while Cal sucked the cum out of the factory workers' balls. By week's end he was swallowing half the workforce. A couple of them were even fucking his ass on a regular basis. It calmed him down and his fidgets subsided.

There was one contingency we overlooked. When the Reverend Callahan turned up at my office, he was so young and good-looking he not only took my breath away but had Gene panting as well. Oh, Cal was going to enjoy this inquisition.

I sent Gene to fetch him while I made us all coffee. The preacher was genial but with little small talk except what was occurring in the minute world of his parish. Sure, he was gorgeous but he was also as boring as bat shit and I was almost nodding off by the time Cal put in an appearance. Gene had obviously advised him of the visitor's striking looks because Cal had not bothered to put on the disguise we had on stand-by. I wondered whether it would work out for the best when I noticed the minister's interest piqued by Cal's appearance.

The small-talk continued although Cal attempted several times to steer it toward more salacious topics. I suggested I vacate my office to leave them to talk together.

"No, I hate to inconvenience you. Besides," he said humbly, "I find it more conducive to private conversation if it's held in less formal surroundings. Do you have a space, a corner somewhere that we can sit where we won't be disturbed?"

"I know just the place," Cal said, jumping to his feet. "Come with me."

I attempted to signal that I didn't think it was a good idea but Cal just ignored me. I knew where they would end up. I also knew Cal would make a pass at the visitor. What I didn't know was whether the preacher would accept the pass or go screaming back to Irene.

There wasn't much I could do to remedy the situation now. I could only wait.

Gene joined me for coffee; we were both nervous of the outcome.

"Who knew the Reverend Callahan would be so hot?" I said.

"Calhoun."

"What?"

"Reverend Calhoun," Gene corrected.

"No, he introduced himself as Callahan."

My blood froze. Gene's face said it all. They had been gone about ten minutes now, plenty of time for…

"Ring the diocese and see if there's a Calhoun or a Callahan and see if one or either is in the vicinity today. If not, ring Roy and Vinnie to get over here immediately."

I raced for the walkway above Cal's trysting area, tripping over my own feet in my hurry. I crept along the metal walkway so they would not be aware I was spying on them. True to form, my son was on his hands and knees and Callahan or whatever his name was had his cock buried in Cal's ass, pulling tightly on his hair, riding him like an animal. Cal's neck was exposed. There was a flow of expletives as Callahan fucked Cal hard, his orgasm obviously building fast. Even faster was the preacher's sleight of hand as he whipped a wire garrote from his pocket and slipped it over Cal's head before tightening it around his neck. Cal fell forward making the noose even tighter, gasping for breath as Callahan continued to ride his ass. I ran back along the metal walkway, my frantic footsteps unheard over Cal's dying gasps. I wrenched the fire extinguisher from the wall before I ran back to position myself over the attempt on my son's life.

"Hey, Callahan," I yelled at the top of my lungs, praying I'd positioned the tank well otherwise it was in danger of crippling Cal.

He looked up just after I'd released the extinguisher and it clocked him square on the nose, before bouncing onto Cal's back. I raced back along the walkway passing my office as Gene shouted, "It's Calhoun who's the minister and he's on leave attending a conference interstate. I've rung Vinnie, he's sending a car."

I didn't stop for any more details and raced down to find Cal clutching his throat, Callahan sprawled behind him. I loosened the garrote to cradle Cal in my arms.

"I'm sorry, dad," he croaked, "I'm always doing the wrong thing."

I hushed him as I heard the siren in the distance. It was becoming a habit. Cal and I were in serious need of new careers.

HAVE SON WILL TRAVEL

"You've obviously seriously pissed off some very dangerous people." Vinnie shook his head having confirmed the dead man, with the ventilation dent where the fire extinguisher I'd dropped from the walkway above had collided with his face, was a contract killer who went by the name of Freddie Pickford. "They won't be pleased you've managed to off poor Freddie, something their rivals haven't managed in twenty years of trying."

The best response I could come up with at the time was "Fuck!"

"Yep, you'll be well and truly fucked when this gets out." Vinnie did like his jokes.

"Then it mustn't get out," Gene said.

"When he doesn't get back to whoever it was hired him, I think they'll have a pretty good idea," Cal added.

"But they won't be sure," Vinnie said. "Freddie was an unstable sorta guy. Not reliable. Genius at what he does best, but you couldn't always rely on him. Drugs is the rumor. Sometimes he'd do a runner, disappear for months on end, then reappear as if nothing had happened."

"Didn't people want their money back?" Gene asked.

Vinnie shrugged. "Freddie just upped his price for the next kill knowing the guy hiring him would deduct the fee for the mission unaccomplished. Simple economics."

"What do we do now?" I asked. "Last thing we need is a police investigation."

"Won't be one of those, mate," Roy assured me. "We consider you've done us all a favor dropping the curtain on this bastard. He's probably the cunt who sliced up Izzy. Leave him to us. He'll just quietly disappear and his employer will think he's done another runner and wait for him to turn up again. Except this time he won't."

Gene was surprised. "You can do that?"

Vinnie tapped the side of his nose. "Don't ask, don't tell."

"Glad you're on our side," Gene smiled sheepishly.

"Won't they send someone else?" Cal sounded concerned.

"Probably," Roy replied.

"That's what I want to talk to you guys about," Vinnie said, lowering his voice in case he was overheard. "You free after we get through with our garbage disposal duties?"

It wasn't a question, it was a demand. Vinnie was serious.

I thought I knew what it was all about and I was way ahead of him. I'd already sent the factory workers home revealing little of what had transpired except to tell them there had been a serious accident. Gene managed to marshal the workers away from the area so no one, as far as we knew, had seen Freddie Pickford's body. The rumor went around, of course, that something had happened to Cal because it was his private area that was suddenly out of bounds. All sorts of conspiracies raged from the sublime to the outright bizarre. The best was that I'd caught Cal and one of the factory hands at it and had lost my temper, injuring the worker so badly he'd been hospitalized. To scotch that one, Cal and I had appeared together when I called a meeting of the staff to tell them to take the remainder of the day off. When the factory hands counted their numbers they realized everyone was present.

With Gene's help I'd concocted a story about some overhead rigging coming loose and falling onto the factory floor. It was convincing enough for the workers to start grousing about getting health and safety in to check the factory's bona fides. I'd get around to addressing that problem in time. Right now I had a life to salvage.

I left the disposal of the body to Roy and Vinnie. The less I knew about it, the safer I felt. Cal was shaken by the incident so he went to lie down until the shock wore off, and he could control his teeth-chattering reaction. I sent Gene and Artie off to a long lunch at my expense to consider the germ of an idea I'd just dropped in their lap, leaving me and Cal alone in the factory. I double checked all points of entry to the building ensuring they were locked. I would have done it anyway but Vinnie insisted. They'd ring on approach when they needed access, while Gene and Artie had their own keys. I also let Lucifer loose to warn of any would-be intruders.

He'd proven a great asset, both as a friend and partner to Cal, and I'd grown attached to the beast. Lucifer must have known my feelings because he allowed me access to Cal's cock and ass with little more than a curious dog smirk unlike the growls and barks that greeted my first attempts when Cal came home from prison and Lucifer had to be banished from the bedroom. He even allowed me to pet him if Cal wasn't around. I was glad to have him on our team; he looked as if he could tear the throat out of any assailant with those powerful jaws.

Lucifer was prowling the factory floor, sniffing the corners, marking his territory when I left him and climbed wearily back up to the office and our makeshift bedroom beyond. Leaving Cal to sleep, I powered up the computer; I had a lot of calculations to work out to see if my plan was viable. Half an hour of financial finagling and I was satisfied so I made a quick call to Vinnie and Roy to check before waking Cal with an ultra-strong coffee.

"We need to talk, son," I said. He sat up in bed, his fine body as seductive an aphrodisiac as ever I'd encountered.

"I know, dad," he said sadly. "I'm bad news. I've caused you nothing but trouble all my life, starting with my visit when I was that arrogant little twat at fourteen. If you'll lend me a few bucks, I'll pack up and clear out. This town's like poison to me now."

I was glad of one half of what he said, at least.

"Where will you go? What will you do?"

"I haven't thought that far ahead. The main thing is to get as far away from you as possible."

I admit it, his words stung me. He must have seen my reaction written large in my face. I couldn't help it. He pulled me to him, enveloping me in his arms.

"No, dad. Not like that. I'm sorry. I put it badly. I love you more than anyone in the world. As my dad and as my lover. But I have to go or I'll drag you down further."

"You've never dragged me anywhere I didn't want to go," I said.

"I could get you killed."

"Answer me a few questions, Cal. Truthfully. Not what you think you should say, or what you think I want to hear. Speak from here." I tapped his chest just above his heart.

"If you'll do the same for me."

I agreed. We both spilled our guts to the extent when Artie and Gene returned some time later they found us

229

both sobbing in each other's arms. They retreated quietly, allowing us privacy to get ourselves in order before we all adjourned to the boardroom where I laid out my ideas as Cal and I wolfed down the lunch they'd brought back with them.

"We don't want you to starve and we didn't think it was a good idea for the two of you to go outside the building today," Gene said.

I don't think either Cal or me knew what we were eating, only that it tasted as good as it smelled and that we didn't leave a single crumb for later.

"That's just it," I said, pushing the plastic container aside, heading to the coffee machine to make us all a new brew. "Cal and I can't live our lives wrapped up in cotton wool, scared at our own shadows, reluctant to leave the factory. That's no life at all. Cal needs to get back to his studies and I need to get on with business. I don't want to have the continual worry of wondering if he's safe. Even if those bastard friends of mine are jailed for their part in Cal's auction, they won't be inside forever."

There was no disagreement from around the table. Artie was quick to pick up on my line of thinking. "You gonna take Roy up on his offer?"

"Cal and I have talked it over and, yeah, we think it's best for both of us. No way do we want to split up, so…"

"What about the company?" Gene always was the practical one.

"Well—"

The word was hardly out of my mouth before Artie interrupted.

"Boss, don't think bad of us but Gene and me have been talking and thinking along the same lines—"

"We weren't plotting anything behind your back," Gene hastened to assure us.

"But we could see your mind was on other things. You was neglecting the business a bit and, well, we…"

"That's not a criticism, Buzz."

I smiled. "I didn't take it that way." This was going better than I had expected. Artie and Gene had obviously discussed it in detail without knowing that our ideas were headed in the same direction.

"We just didn't know how to bring up the subject," Gene added. "What with you preoccupied and Cal in jail."

Artie finally managed to get it off his chest. "We want to buy the company, Buzz."

Cal had remained quiet through the discussion, but now he was beaming. "Great minds think alike."

"You guys were thinking the same?" Artie asked.

We both nodded enthusiastically.

Gene's conservative side kicked in. "Of course, we can't offer the same as you would get from some of the big companies that are just looking to gobble up your assets."

I pushed the paperwork I had printed from my computer calculations across the table to him. Gene and Artie went into a huddle, whispering to each other. There was much nodding of heads while I gave them space by going to pour us all coffee. When I brought the tray back with the mugs and the pot, my two workers could scarcely contain their Cheshire cat grins.

"You know it's worth a lot more than that?" Gene said, tapping a figure at the bottom of the page.

"A fucking shed load more," Artie added. "I know what your future orders are Buzz, even if you don't realize yet."

"I realize all right, Artie. I've been preoccupied, I haven't been asleep at the wheel."

"Sorry, boss."

Gene wasn't about to be deflected. "You'd really sell to us for this amount?"

"Uh huh."

Artie was suddenly concerned. "You wouldn't take the money and set up in opposition to us somewhere else?"

I laughed. "Artie, the first place those murderous bastards will come looking for us is in the same industry. It's a no brainer. I'm out for good."

"Sorry, I had to ask."

"We've already approached the bank about a loan," Gene admitted.

"I know," I smiled. "They rang me about it, to see if the company was for sale. Wondering if there was something they should know, like if I was going bad."

"Bastards," Artie spat.

Gene was more placatory. "They were only looking after their interests."

"Will they come to the party?" I asked.

"Almost," Gene said. "We don't need a lot more so we can raise the rest but it will leave us short for the running of the factory for about six months."

I had a request. "Do me a favor. Ask Roy and Vinnie if they'd like to come onboard. I owe them big time and I suspect they wouldn't mind a bit of diversification with some of their hard-earned cash. I wouldn't be surprised if they both had a nice nest egg stashed away somewhere safe for a rainy day. And it wouldn't be enough they could tell you what to do, you'd both still be in charge."

"Plus it wouldn't hurt to have two guys like Bert and Ernie on side," Cal added, referencing *Sesame Street*, his favorite program as a child.

We were celebrating prematurely when the cops themselves rang to say they were on approach. I guess the four of us were a little merry when they arrived because they could scarcely believe in our change of attitude from that morning.

I poured them a tumbler of their favorite booze each and raised my glass. "To freedom."

They repeated the toast before we all knocked back our drinks and Gene poured another round.

"You've decided then?" Roy asked.

I nodded.

"What about all this?" Vinnie asked, indicating the building in which we were all getting pissed.

"That's the good news, guys," I slurred. "To the prospective new owners, Gene and Artie."

We toasted again.

"We just have to find a couple of small investors to get us over the initial hump," Gene hinted, winking at me. "Then it will all be rosy."

"Just how much is this little hump?" Vinnie asked, feigning indifference.

Gene put his arm around the cop, maneuvering him into a quiet corner. The price must have been to Vinnie's liking because he called Roy aside to join the discussion. They both emerged from the scrum looking well pleased with the result.

Roy got serious before we all lost our sense of perspective. "I don't think you should stay here any longer," he warned. He'd taken me aside for a private chat. "It's okay being here during the day while the workers are about but you and Cal are much too vulnerable after dark." He handed me a number of keys attached to a Rolls-Royce insignia. "That's my dream," he said when he saw my look of surprise. He scribbled an address on the back of his cop business card. "It's a bit out of town but it's like a fuckin' fortress. You'd need a ballistic missile to get you buggers out once you're inside. Take my car, as well. No one will hassle you in that. Most bastards recognize the number and give it a wide berth. They're obviously a little too familiar with yours for comfort. I'll organize all the rest. Get you a new car through official channels and get the ball rolling with regards to the witness protection. Cal will still have to come back to testify against your former friends, but he'll be safe away from here until then."

"Thanks mate. I owe you big time."

Roy got that mischievous smile that was a dead giveaway. "Okay, son, the cops are on your tail, how do you want them?"

There was a hoot from everyone in the room as Cal quickly removed his clothes before greasing his asshole with a pump container of lube I kept in the boardroom for such parties. We celebrated the forthcoming deals by nailing Cal to the table, all taking turns fucking his ass until it was running like ripe quadruple cream camembert. I watched, not at all envious that Cal was having the time of his life with other men, my cock hard as the steel rods on the factory floor.

Vinnie and Artie lined up for seconds but I still hadn't blown my load. I was saving that for alone time. I'd jam a butt plug in Cal's ass later to keep the spunk fermenting in his bowels. Late in the evening, as we were getting ready to leave, I told Gene that as far as I was concerned, he and Artie could take charge as of the next day. I'd be in to sign contracts and pay wages and shit like that until they could get the loan in place. We all thought it would be a good idea to keep negotiations secret, we didn't want to show our hand as yet, and meanwhile Cal and I would start making our arrangements.

"Hey, guys, before you all leave, there's one last thing I have to do."

The others paused. They didn't see the bombshell coming.

"Cal," I said as I slipped onto one knee. "I love you, mate. I love you more and more each day. You broaden my horizons at every opportunity and I'm telling you now, if you say 'yes' I will always protect you and I will never let you go, no matter what. Cal, will you marry me?"

Our state didn't allow same-gender marriage but I'd already had a word to old Judge Upton and he was prepared to overlook that fact plus the obvious deterrent to the solemnization of our marriage vows because we were father and son, in exchange for participating in something so perverse it got him hard. It also meant he got to participate in Cal's ass.

The room waited expectantly. Cal pulled some sort of face which he must have thought approximated pondering the question. I didn't know what I would do if he responded negatively.

When he did finally answer I saw he'd taken his time because there were tears in his eyes and he was choked up. "I'd be honored to marry you, dad."

We went into a group hug that seemed to last for ages, everyone talking at once, eager to pass on their congratulations. I explained about Upton doing the honors in a private ceremony to which they were all invited as would be Izzy and Derek. Date to be notified. The party broke up shortly afterwards.

By the time we reached Roy's weekender on the outskirts of the city, the single story bungalow undetectable from its neighbors, its backyard rolling down an expanse of lawn to the edge of a lake with a small wooden jetty, Cal and I were both exhausted but not too tired that I didn't have the inclination to extract the spunk from his reddened ass with my mouth, dribbling it into his own until our kisses had sucked him dry, our mouths as slimy as snail mucous on a concrete path. Then I fucked his swollen hole until he shot his load all over his chest and onto his own face, scooping it up on my fingers, feeding it to him as I dumped the last load of the day deep inside him.

It was the best night's sleep either of us had experienced in quite a while, the next day spent with me on the phone setting up appointments and preparing paperwork while Cal swam off the end of the jetty then sunned himself on the lawn out of sight of any prying neighbors. He came in to make a light lunch for the two of us then invited me to join him later in the afternoon for a relaxing dip. By about 3pm I was free to do as he wanted and we whooped and hollered like two teenagers, scaring a number of pelicans that were lazily scooping for fish near the shore.

I prayed this was what our new life could be like. And, too, that Cal wouldn't get too stir crazy confined to this house and its surrounds. I needn't have worried, especially after Izzy and Derek came out to spend a weekend. I'd filled them in briefly on recent events and they agreed we didn't have much choice if we wanted our relationship to survive. Izzy was almost back to his old self and a weekend of lazing about in the sun was just what the doctor ordered. We discovered Roy had a row boat stored away in an old shed on his property and the three of them took it out on the lake while I continued to get my business affairs in order.

We'd also decided to have the wedding here in this haven of tranquility and made arrangements that everyone would be put up for the night, except for Judge Upton who had to get back to the city. I don't think any of us were fussed by that. Gene had kept the business running smoothly, sprouting the official line that I had taken a well-deserved holiday from the business and would return the following month.

The wedding day dawned warm and sunny, the lake flat and placid as it lapped the moorings at the end of the yard. Gene and Artie were bringing Izzy and Derek and the catering which I'd ordered to be delivered to the factory, Roy bringing anything that didn't fit in Artie's car, while Vinnie was responsible for the grog.

We dressed up for the occasion, Cal and I in identically tailored suits, the others making an effort to the best of their financial ability. None of us cared particularly but I wanted me and Cal to look good in the photographs, after all it was a big step for both of us. Otherwise we all knew we wouldn't be in our clothes for long.

I'd written my own vows and Cal had done the same so as we'd had no rehearsal they came as a surprise not only to the guests but to each other as well. Marriage vows are such a personal thing that what sounds heartfelt and moving to participants probably sounds mawkish and sentimental to outsiders but there were no dry eyes by the time Cal and I had both said 'I do.'

The judge solemnly intoned, "By the power vested in me, I now declare you husband and husband." He could scarcely conceal his delight at being able to add, "You may now fuck the groom." He was somewhat chastened to find he had to wait until the wedding photographs were taken by Derek who was a deft hand with a digital camera, although Upton quite wisely declined to appear with us. Then the clothes came off, the judge did a bit of wham bam and was off having fulfilled his duty as well as having filled Cal's ass. The remainder of the evening and all the next day passed in a haze of sexual excess, not all of it concentrated on Cal's ass.

This was meant to be a joyous occasion and there was none of the frantic rutting than accompanied most Cal gangbangs. In fact, Derek and I spent some time together and Izzy managed to plug my ass on more than one occasion. The only two who didn't give up their butts were the two ostensibly straight cops, Vinnie and Roy. They did, however, branch out on this occasion and shared their cocks equally with Derek and Izzy.

There was so much cum shooting out of stiff pricks I thought we'd have to hose the place down. We were all sated by the Sunday afternoon as the other six members of the wedding party got ready to leave, although I sensed Cal was not really satisfied. His appetites were more degraded than joyous although he could do both but like a diet of too many carbs, you sometimes need variety.

The wheels of the law turn slowly and both Cal and I were getting jittery. I'd done all I could to hurry up the transfer of title to the business, it was now just a case of awaiting the lawyers on both sides. The bank had come through with the loan, as had Roy and Vinnie with their shares, the witness protection was in place ready to take effect as soon as the money situation was finalized.

The most excitement we had in the weeks following my clearing out of our old home which was then put on the market, selling quickly below its true value, was discovering the new names we'd been allocated. Cal loathed them on hearing. We were officially listed as Ben and Paul Philips.

"We sound like fuckin' puppets on a kids' Saturday morning television show," Cal whined.

I had to agree but there was little we could do about it. The powers that be had also decided to send us to a small city known for its violence against gay men. I began to wonder whether they wanted us dead.

"You just have to play it low key until the trial is over," Vinnie said after another of Cal's critical rants. But I didn't think the two cops looked happy about it either.

We were a pair of ungrateful bastards I suppose complaining that things weren't moving fast enough, that we hated our new names which, try as we might using them at home, we always fell back to using Buzz and Cal. The new names didn't suit so they didn't stick.

In due course, our departure date arrived. We'd spent the previous evening sobbing our goodbyes with Izzy,

Derek, Artie and Gene. Suddenly it all felt so final, like we would never see them again. But we would when we turned up for the trial. We couldn't reveal where we were headed or what our new names were which made our farewells that much more difficult. There was no way we could keep in touch with our friends.

Our final morning, Roy and Vinnie turned up with our 'new' car courtesy of witness protection, so new it would be untraceable to us under our old names. We now had to embrace the new, or perish. The car was a second-hand Japanese make, so generic in color and design that it was instantly camouflaged the moment it hit the streets as so many other vehicles were of similar make and shading. The beige interior was as modest as everything about the vehicle.

"You won't draw attention to yourself that way," Vinnie claimed.

"Beige? Who chose it? Some color-blind cop at headquarters? Some design-impaired bureaucrat?" Cal was in full fury.

"I'm afraid you're stuck with it until the trial is over," Roy said.

Sometimes I wished we'd just skipped town and set up life in a distant city although I knew without new identities we'd be easily tracked by anyone wishing us harm. But it was hard to be grateful at times.

Vinnie handed me a card. "This is the garage that does all police work. Get the car a final check-up, you've got a long drive ahead of you. Top up the tank as well. Police Department expense."

"I suppose it will get us there in one piece?" I asked facetiously.

Our farewells to the two cops who had saved us on more than one occasion was a solemn affair. There was no way we could ever repay their kindness although they didn't seem to care too much about that. They were full of good advice and warnings, fussing over us like old chooks.

We had little to load into the car as we were beginning again, so we had the minimum of personal items about us, plus a great deal more manufactured personal items for our new life, including bank accounts, driver's licenses, tax file numbers – you name it, we had it. I'd never been so organized in my life before. As we drove away, I couldn't help but feel some slight excitement at our new life. I would have to find a job, Cal would enroll in a new university, particularly as Roy had managed to manipulate higher marks in Paul Philips's exam results than Cal had ever achieved as himself. It meant he could now study just about anything he wanted, provided he had no dreams of being a doctor or a lawyer. Still, that left the field wide open.

I had a folder full of personal and business references that would open doors but as I'd been in the one business all my life I wasn't sure what appealed. We were still excitedly discussing our prospects when I pulled into the garage. Vinnie told me to drive straight inside and that we'd be taken care of immediately.

There were three grease monkeys working on a vehicle on the hoist when we arrived. A big gorilla of a man wearing overalls sauntered over, wiping his hands on a rag as oily as the floor. I got out of the car, meeting his firm grip with one of equal strength.

"You must be Ben Philips," he said smirking.

I didn't know the protocol about whether he knew the names were fake so I just agreed.

"That's my boy, Paul." I knocked the bonnet of the car to draw Cal's attention because he was staring at the two mechanics farther into the garage. He nodded at the gorilla I was talking to, running his eyes quite obviously up the guy's body which was impressively muscular that even his dirty overalls could not disguise it.

"Could you just check the car's in good running order and fill the tank?"

"Will do. I'll get the boys on it right away."

"Is it okay if Paul stays with the car? I have to get some bank shit cleared up. Where's the nearest?"

The gorilla shrugged. "Sure, why not?" He gave me directions to the bank which was quite a hike away but it was a balmy day and the walk would do me good.

I informed Cal I would be gone about an hour and that he was okay to stay with the car. He seemed more than happy to do so. I walked out into the street, heading off in the direction I'd been told, but doubling around the block coming back to the garage from the opposite direction. As I suspected, I'd been steered away from the bank just around the corner. The garage boss wanted me out of the way. Sometimes it pays to have a suspicious disposition.

The garage bay roller door had been closed since I left which conjured up various scenarios, the one I hoped most applicable being the one that involved Cal's ass. Anything else was too hideous to contemplate. I tried the door to the front office but it was locked. I didn't dare try to lift the shutter so I squeezed down the tight passageway between the garage and the building next door. Luck was with me and the small bathroom window was wide open. It was easy enough to use the adjoining wall to caterpillar my way up the side of the building to slither through the narrow bathroom window. It was a tight fit and I grazed my arm badly.

The sounds I made as I jumped down into the small lavatory were loud enough to attract attention, but I guess traffic noise and the garage radio spewing out loud rap was enough to disguise my break-in. Opening the door quietly, I found I was at the back of the premises, with a view down to where Cal was still seated in the car while chatting to the two mechanics as they examined the engine. The gorilla was in his glass windowed office talking animatedly to someone on the phone.

The place was dark enough that I could creep along the wall toward the office without being seen although I wasn't sure I'd be invisible if the gorilla turned to look in my direction, his attention currently focused on the car. I made a dash for it, my heart in my throat, not overly concerned if I was seen as I could always say I'd tried the door and found it locked and entered via the bathroom because we were in a hurry. No, I wanted to listen in on the conversation. Something wasn't right here.

"Yeah, they arrived about ten minutes ago. Sure, it's the car description you gave me." He listed the number, the make and the color. "The dad has gone off to the bank. I steered him to one that's a good half hour away. Gave him shit directions. He'll be gone a while. No, the kid's in the car. Not a big deal, he looks like he wouldn't know a carburetor from a petrol cap. No shit! He does that? Hey, we're no fags but...hold on. Bob, come here, mate."

One of the mechanics came into the office.

"Yeah boss."

"Listen, when you get through with the brakes, they only gotta last for fifty miles or so, best they fail around the Pass. Got it?"

"Yeah."

"The kid in the car. Faggot. Best piece of ass ever. Best blow job ever. According to..." The boss nodded in the direction of the phone.

Shit. He was talking to someone who knew Cal, who had fucked Cal. I immediately thought of Roy and Vinnie. Nah, couldn't be. I cursed to myself that the boss hadn't used his caller's name.

"You sayin' me and Dutch can do him over?"

"As rough as you like," the boss said. "But make sure you take care of things first."

"No sweat." Bob seemed eager to get back to the job.

"Looks like the guys are gonna give him a farewell bang," the boss chuckled down the phone. "No, nothing can go wrong this end. Yeah, I saw the license. Ben Philips. The dad said his son's name was Paul. It all checks out so stop worrying. You're giving me an ulcer. No, I can't guarantee he'll go over the edge. That's your job."

The phone call which gleaned me no further information ended with, "Gotta go, mate. Gotta get me some of that fine fag ass."

I waited until he was out of the office then crept back along the wall to the sounds of "Suck it, fag!" and the sound of Cal choking. I had no doubt he'd handle himself like the good young slut he was.

Back in the bathroom, the sound echoed as I dialed my mobile phone but I knew they were making enough noise outside it was unlikely they'd hear me. I did take the precaution of whispering.

"Roy, it's Ben. Ben Philips." For a moment I thought he hadn't recognized the name. "You were right all along. Checking the car, working over Paul as we speak. No, not like that, the usual. Yeah, I think they'll be at it for a while yet. Most I can string it out is about forty-five minutes to an hour. Sounds like it's meant to happen around about the Pass down the coast. Fifty miles. Okay. And thanks, you're a regular life saver."

I had nothing to do but find a spot in the garage hidden from the mechanics' sight and watch Cal get a right buggering. They'd finished what they had to do with the engine because the hood was down and the three guys were naked apart from their boots and socks, spearing their cocks into Cal's mouth one after the other as he kneeled in the dirt and grease.

The boss wanted more and lifted Cal, pushing him face down over the hood, smearing his butt with some sort of grease. Like a jack hammer he thrust his prick roughly between Cal's cheeks until my son bellowed in pain.

"Shut the fuck up, slut," the boss said ramming my son's head down on the bonnet of the car. "I've been told you love cock and you love it rough so that's how we're giving it to you. Any objections, cunt?"

There was no objection from Cal because his mouth had been impaled on Dutch's cock after he scrambled to sit on the bonnet. They took turns fucking his ass, passing him around like he was a slab of fuck meat, slapping him, thrusting in his throat until he gagged, in his ass until the breath was knocked out of him. They called him every foul name they could lay their tongues to which I knew would only turn Cal on all the more. If they thought they were humiliating him they were lousy mind readers.

I watched for a good half hour as they squirted load after load into him, adjusting my own cock as it hardened. I didn't want to blow my load here, I'd save it for later, knowing the more Cal gets the more he wants. He was practically begging them to fuck him again.

"Shit, you really are some fag slut, aren't you boy? Pity we ain't got time to invite some of the boys over, they'd love to get stuck into an ass like yours. Some of them got cocks that would rip you open," the boss snorted.

"What we gonna tell his dad?" Bob asked.

"Just that his precious little son slipped over in a pool of oil when he got outa the car. You'll agree with that, won't you fag? Unless you want us to give the same treatment to your dad and then bury the evidence on a building site."

Cal agreed to tell the lie.

"Go and get yourself washed up a bit, fag," the boss yelled.

I had to get out of there before Cal or one of the mechanics discovered me. Slipping into the toilet I scrambled onto the bowl and hoisted myself through the window. As I slithered down the outside wall I heard Cal enter the bathroom and turn on the taps to give himself a cat wash. He was humming.

By the time I got to the end of the passageway, the roller shutter was up again and Bob and Dutch were back at work on the car they were repairing when I first arrived. The boss came out of his office when I strode back inside.

"Your son's had a bit of an accident," he said.

"Nothing serious, I hope."

"Slipped in a pool of oil. Bit of a cut to his face, and his clothes are a bit greasy but he's fine."

"Where is he?"

"Just washing up in the rest room."

I signed the paperwork and by the time I got back to the car, Cal was already aboard ready to head out.

"Have a safe journey," the hypocrite boss called as I drove away.

Cal was quiet for the first few blocks, then amazed me when he said, "They tampered with the car, didn't they?"

"Yep."

He digested the news.

"So it's likely Phil knows our new names, our new car, and will be waiting for us somewhere."

"The Pass down the coast road," I said.

Cal laughed. "You watched them fuck me, didn't you?"

"I sure did. Enjoy yourself?"

"I sure did!"

We were laughing still as we headed out of town toward our not-so-secret-anymore new lives, although I was taking the journey very slow and steady, watching the road to see if we were being tailed.

Cal slept for the most part after I made sure he strapped himself in with his seat belt. We made good time along the expressway, once we left the crowded streets of the town behind.

The plan was to take it very easy on the treacherous mountain pass where numerous lives had been lost to drink as cars didn't make hairpin bends and careened through the metal barrier onto the trees and rocks below, obviously where the mechanics intended us to lose our lives. It was also an area in which the owners of clapped-out cars brought them to push over the side in an effort to claim insurance once they'd reported them stolen.

With the final exit that led to the bypass of the mountain road behind us, I spied a police car half-hidden in the bushes at the side of the road where they always waited to catch drunk drivers. Much as I would have liked to, we couldn't use the detour as it would take us thirty miles out of our way. There was only one way for us to go. I glanced in the rear view mirror and saw the cop car pull out of its semi-hiding place. Within seconds the driver had thrown barricades up across the road so no vehicle could follow us. That told me we were in deep shit.

I kept my eyes peeled for anything unusual, like the fact there was no oncoming traffic. I knew the road behind us was blocked so someone must have done the same ahead of us. It mattered little now if we turned back or continued on our way, we were caught in a pincer movement. I kept the car at a steady speed so if the brakes failed, as they would inevitably, I could steer into the rock face at the side of the road rather than over the embankment. That was in case they hadn't something more sinister in mind.

We knew now that Phil had powerful friends in important positions, including the treacherous bastard in the police force who had discovered our subterfuge. I was nervous as hell, and glad that Cal was sleeping. In fact, it came as a relief when I finally confronted the inevitable roadblock.

I slowed the car, bringing it to a halt just in front of the police car stationed across the roadway. I recognized the cop immediately he stepped out in front of us. Con, the Drug Squad goon who had fucked Cal on film.

"Stay in the car, sir. Keep your hands where I can see them."

I did as I was told, noticing there was no one with Con. His partner must be the car at the other end of the roadblock.

"Place your hands on the steering wheel, sir."

There was no point resisting although I knew I'd be cuffed making it even more difficult to escape.

The sound of voices had awoken Cal who still seemed a bit dazed as he got out of the passenger's side to ask what was going on.

"Nothing to concern yourself with, slut," Con said viciously. "We have an all points alert out that you have one of the most fuckable asses in the country and we have a man who would dearly love to do just that, fuck it, before said ass is fried."

Phil emerged from the shadows behind us, obviously the man I'd seen throw up the road block. He'd walked down to ensure we didn't escape, his face an evil mask.

"You two lead a charmed life," he sneered, "although the charm is totally beyond me. Unless, of course, we're talking about this fag's butthole." He patted Cal on the ass, before grabbing his wrists and cuffing them behind his back, pushing him roughly into a kneeling position.

"The two of us are gonna fuck you, boy. Fuck you in front of your own father. You're gonna beg us to do you or we'll fucking make his death so painful it'll make the angels weep. Your dad is gonna die, boy, you can make it easy on him or make it painful. The choice is yours. What's it to be?"

"I'll co-operate," Cal said. "I'll come with you if you let him go."

"You're in no position to bargain. We could kill him and just take you with us."

"Wouldn't you like it better if I'm co-operative?"

"Nah, who cares?" Phil said, slamming the back of his hand across Cal's cheek. "In fact, I'd really prefer it if you struggle. More pleasure for me and Con."

All I could do was watch in horror as Phil hauled out his cock and shoved it brutally down Cal's throat holding the back of his head until my son looked as if he were about to pass out.

Much as I hated to do it, I kept mum, not giving them the satisfaction of pleading. I knew it would be of no use.

Con opened the passenger door, wriggled out of his regulation trousers and sat beside me, his cock hard as his police baton.

"Suck it, boy," Phil demanded, pulling Cal up by his hair then pushing his face onto Con's blood-filled prick. Cal's trousers were pulled down and Phil pushed his fingers into his ass, snorting with pleasure. "I see the boys at the garage worked you over. Bet your dad didn't know about that, did he? Did daddy know his precious little son was fucked senseless by the garage mechanics while he went on a wild goose chase trying to find a bank?"

Phil spat in his hand a number of times then slathered the saliva over his cock before ramming it into my boy's guts pushing his face down on Con's cock so he choked.

"I guess I'll disappoint you then, Phil. I watched the whole gangbang. Oh, I might have missed the first few moments because I was busy listening to the phone call that the boss of the operation was obviously putting through to your mate, Con. I saw the boss slam Cal's face onto the hood and I saw them take turns fucking his ass using grease as the lubricant. I even heard them make up the lie to explain how beat up Cal looked. He supposedly slipped in a pool of grease."

That gave Con pause. I saw the exchange of worried looks between him and Phil.

"Bullshit," Phil snapped, although he sounded anything but convincing. "If you heard that then you'd know they tampered with the brakes."

"Yep, knew that as well."

"Crap! You would have swapped the car."

"Oh, didn't I tell you that we did. Check the engine. You see, Phil, the advantage of a nondescript car like this is you can swap the plates and no one realizes. The one the guys tampered with at the garage has been impounded. I think you might be in dire need of a new mechanic next time your car needs servicing."

Con was not at all happy with the way the conversation was going and he tried to pull Cal off his cock although Cal was having none of it and suctioned like a vacuum cleaner.

"So what's the plan, Phil? Knock us both out, lock us in the car and send us off the roadway?"

"Doesn't matter whether we do it or you do it yourselves, either way it's a win/win situation for us."

"So much planning, Phil, and it's all come unraveled."

"I don't like this," Con said, yanking Cal's mouth off his dick. "Let's get this show on the road."

He shoved Cal, knocking Phil over onto the asphalt. The cop pulled up his trousers and before Phil could regain his feet, had unbuckled his gun from its holster.

"Time to say bye bye, dumbass," Con smiled as he aimed at my head.

Gritting my teeth, I prepared for the worst, time slowing so that a second seemed like ten, until I heard a scream of pain and the snarl of a cherished friend. Con was on the ground, Lucifer's jaws wrapped around his wrist, his gun in easy reach of Phil who put his hand out to grab it. Cal was quick enough to kick it under the car.

Purple with rage, Phil put his fists around Cal's neck and began to throttle him.

"Lucifer, help Cal. Help Cal," I said.

The dog looked at me and I nodded my head toward Phil. The dog pounced and Phil let go immediately as Lucifer wrapped his jaws around his leg.

That's how Roy and Vinnie found us a few minutes later, Lucifer having subdued Con and Phil, standing guard over them, snarling and drooling as if he'd like to have them for dinner. Vinnie uncuffed me while Roy attended to Cal who was hacking his lungs out at the side of the road. Once freed I went over to comfort him with Roy and Vinnie.

Unfortunately, Con had reached the security of the police car and was doing a bunk at high speed. Phil was close behind as I'd left the keys to my car in the ignition and while our attention was distracted.

"They won't get far," Vinnie assured us. "We made a few modifications to the police car while we were watching what was going on."

I shrugged. "And Phil thinks I changed the plates for a safer car that hadn't been tampered with. Wonder how he'll feel when he discovers I lied."

Of course, we were never to find out. Phil was too dead by half when they retrieved his body from the bottom of a ravine after he lost control and went over the side. Nor could we ask Con if he had any idea as he'd attempted to steer a course away from the edge and had slammed at high speed into an inconveniently placed tree at the side of the road. His car burst into flames.

We only found out about it in the newspapers the following day under the banner headline HORROR HIGHWAY: TWO DEAD.

Roy pulled into a busy 24-hour gas station with adjacent café and we sat and ate for the first time since we'd set out. Vinnie had enough on his plate for five full-grown men.

"Vinnie," I said, "If you don't start eating healthy you'll end up dead by the time you're fifty."

"Let him alone, dad. He and Roy saved us. They deserve anything they want."

Roy reached into the satchel he'd brought with him, handing me a pile of papers.

"New identity, new tax file numbers, new bank account. By the way I transferred the money from the factory sale into the account through such a circuitous route it would take a Rubik to track it down. As far as the authorities are concerned Ben and Paul Philips have disappeared off the face of the earth. You are now Ian and Brock Green—"

"Brock." Cal tried it out on his tongue and we all held our breath. "Hey, I like it. Brock Green."

Finally, Roy held out his hand. It contained car keys to yet another nondescript vehicle in the car park.

"Good luck guys. Wherever you end up think of us every now and then," Vinnie smiled.

"We'll never forget you guys."

They got into the police car and left without looking back.

"So dad," Cal could barely contain his glee.

"Yes Brock."

"Does this mean we don't have the nasty business of having to return for the court case?"

"Nope," I said. "It means Clive and Zach will probably walk free. But who cares, eh?"

I must admit I checked under the hood before I got in the car, but I didn't really know what I was looking for. I headed back in the direction we'd come. We'd drive until we found somewhere that looked promising, or maybe keep traveling indefinitely.

As it turned out we did find a city we liked the second week of our adventures. Large enough to disappear into, beautiful parks and facilities and with sufficient new high-rise apartment buildings that we could remain anonymous if we wanted to. We stayed in a classy hotel as Cal slowly worked his way through the male staff until we found a luxurious apartment with a view of the river and the city from the sun deck. The apartment itself was spacious and modern, enough bedrooms that we could have guests although the third bedroom was more likely to become Cal's study. He had his own bedroom in case either of us entertained on our own. More importantly, they allowed dogs.

He fell in love with it the moment he saw it, impatiently waiting for the exchange of contracts.

I supervised the furnishings while Cal sifted through courses at the uni, until the day I stopped to pick him up in a flashy red sports car.

"Where did you get that?" Cal asked as I pulled up in front of him.

"Hop in, I have a surprise."

He had no idea where we were headed until I pressed the remote and drove into the underground car park of our new home, Midwich Park Towers. I'd moved our few personal items out of the hotel, and into the apartment.

As we shot up in the elevator, a male with a chest as big as Dolly Parton's and the looks of a Colin Farrell got in at ground level. I almost had to push Cal's tongue back in his mouth. The stud turned back and smiled as he got out of the lift the floor below ours.

I unlocked the door to our apartment, grabbing Cal before he could barge in. I lifted him in my arms like a bride and kissed him.

I kicked open the door, Lucifer bounding to greet us.

"You think we should invite that guy who shared the lift with us up for drinks?" Cal said, "It'd be rude not to get to know the neighbors."

I laughed as I carried Cal into the apartment and the true start of our new life.

"Son, don't ever change."

ABOUT THE AUTHOR

Barry Lowe writes about love and sex so he won't forget how to do it. Born in Sydney, he and his partner of 45 years now live in Malta where their relationship is legally recognised.

He began writing stories when he was about ten and the ideas still haven't stopped popping into his head although his fingers aren't as nimble as they once were.

In between writing romance fiction he penned a biography of 1950s blonde diva actress, Mamie Van Doren, published by McFarland as Atomic Blonde. Mostly he writes about love's wonderful variations for a series of eBooks, novels and anthologies for Lydian Press.

He also writes bisexual stories as Jazmin Starr and gritty gay noir as Tal Dagger.

Check out his website at www.barrylowe.net.

OTHER WORKS BY BARRY LOWE

PLAYS

Available in eBook and Print

THE DEATH OF PETER PAN: Gay Historical Romance

NOVELS & ANTHOLOGIES

Available in eBook and Print

BUSTING BILLY'S BUTT: A Gay Erotic Romance

Steve and Billy's monogamous relationship has gone stale until Billy, ever the exhibitionist, shows them a way to spice up their sex life.

THE MAJOR AND THE MINERS: A Gay Historical Romance

1930s Australia: Two men from opposite ends of the social spectrum. Is love enough to overcome the obstacles between them?

THE GRAVY TRAIN: A Murder Mystery with Recipes

Someone on the train has an appetite for murder!

A TOUCH OF THE SON: A Gay Novel

Their secret passion will lead them to hell. Will they be able to find their way back?

ROMANCING THE BONE: Gay Romance Erotica

OMG! NOT ANOTHER GAY EROTICA ANTHOLOGY?

ROUGH & READY: Gay Tough Guy Erotica

YOUR BOYFRIEND IS HOT: Gay Cuckold Erotica

BEAR SKIN: Hot Gay Bear Erotica

THE MORE THE MERRIER: Gay Gangbang Erotica

THE BOY IS A BOTTOM: Gay Anal Erotica

COCK-EYED OPTIMISTS: Gay Romance Erotica

BABY, I'M NOT A MONSTER: Gay Vampire and Other Paranormal Erotica

CHRISTMAS CRACKER: Gay Erotica for the Holidays

BUTT BOYS: Gay Anal Erotica

BACHELOR BOY

BAD-ASS BOYS

EVERYTHING'S COMING UP ROSES

THE BI-WORD

SELECTED SHORT FICTION

Available as eBooks

SOLD BY MY STEPDAD

HOMO FOR THE HOLIDAYS

LOVE WITH A SIDE ORDER OF PELICANS

CHRISTMAS IN JULY

BREEDING MY BOYFRIEND

NEW JOCK IN TOWN

BACHELOR BOY

SUMMER AT RAINBOW COVE

I WAS A MALE NYMPHO FOR THE FBI

HOW MUCH IS THAT DOGGIE IN THE WINDOW?

THE DAY OF THE CLIFFORDS

HE WON'T SEND ROSES

PRIDE AND JOY

THE GOOD, THE BAD, AND THE CUDDLY

THE GROOM CLOSET

HARD ON HIS HEELS

THE NEW DAD'S CLUB

For all Barry's titles please visit his page at: lydianpress.com